AN HEIR IS MISPLACED

A DUCHESS OF STORTFORD MYSTERY

HELEN GOLDEN

DREW BRADLEY PRESS

BOOKS BY HELEN GOLDEN

The Duchess of Stortford Mysteries

An Heir is Misplaced (Novella)

A Husband is Hushed Up

A Right Royal Cozy Investigation Series

A Toast To Trouble (Novella)

Tick, Tock, Mystery Clock (Novella)

Spruced Up For Murder

For Richer, For Deader

Not Mushroom For Death

An Early Death (Prequel)

Deadly New Year (Novella)

A Dead Herring

I Spy With My Little Die

A Cocktail to Die For

Dying To Bake

A Death of Fresh Air

I Kill Always Love You

Murder Most Wilde

ISBN (P) 978-1-915747-35-8

Edited by Marina Grout at Writing Evolution

Published by Drew Bradley Press

Cover design by Helen Drew-Bradley

First edition June 2025

Note from the Author

NOTE FROM THE AUTHOR

I am a British author and this book has been written using British English. So if you are from somewhere other than the UK, you may find some words spelt differently to how you would spell them. In most cases this is British English, not a spelling mistake. We also have different punctuation rules in the UK. However if you find any other errors I would be grateful if you would please contact me helen@helengolde nauthor.co.uk and let me know so I can correct them. Thank you.

You will see the phrase 'the *ton*' used occasionally in this book. *Ton* means 'fashionable society,' particularly high class society, and comes from *le bon ton*, a French phrase meaning 'good or elegant form or style.' Members of the *ton* were generally upper class, wealthy, and respected. By the late 19th century the phrase was considered a little old-fashioned so although it was still used by the older and more traditional members of society, younger people referred to 'society' or 'high society' instead.

For your reference I have included a list of characters in the order they appear and you can find this at the back of the book.

1

MONDAY 18 MAY 1891

The incessant patter of rain against the glass only deepened Alice's, The Duchess of Stortford's, sense of malaise. Her eyes flitted across the morning room at Darby House, past the slightly drooping indoor ferns that mirrored her current spirits, and settled on the increasingly blurred lines of Grosvenor Square through the large window. *Will this rain ever stop?* Three days of relentless rain, and the whole of London society appeared to have come to a standstill. Daytime engagements were postponed; no one wished to venture out into the rivers of mud and manure that the roads and pathways had become.

She sighed as she glanced down at the table by the side of the sofa she was lounging on and picked up *Lippincott's Monthly Magazine*. She leafed idly through the pages. Nothing interested her. Not even the latest instalment of Oscar Wilde's *The Picture of Dorian Gray*, with its high drama and decadence, could tempt her. She set it back onto the table with another sigh and picked up the broadsheet that had been underneath, *The Society Page*.

Although in public, Alice described *The Society Page* as,

"vulgar and irreverent", in private she was an avid reader of the scandal sheet. Her heart sank as she read the headline: *Is the Duke of Stortford Carrying On?* She heaved another sigh as she continued to read:

It has come to the attention of this publication that His Grace, the Duke of Stortford, may be conducting himself with undue familiarity in the company of Lady Forthington—the recently widowed and not inconsolable neighbour to Manning Hall, the Duke's country seat in Derbyshire.

The lady in question, the widow of the late Sir Francis Forthington, is none other than a niece of His Grace the Duke of Arnwall and thus cousin to Her Grace the Duchess of Stortford. Having only just emerged from mourning for her late husband—an older gentleman of means—Lady Forthington now appears intent on embracing the privileges of widowhood with commendable enthusiasm.

It is whispered in certain drawing rooms that Her Grace, the Duchess of Stortford, who is presently residing in London and seen frequently in Mayfair society, has thus far turned a discreet blind eye to her husband's rural diversions. Yet one wonders how long such forbearance may continue, particularly given the familial connection and the evident proximity of the lady in question.

Will the Duchess journey north to reclaim her place at Manning Hall and assert her position anew? Or shall she elect to remain in Town, allowing matters to unfold as they may? Society watches with no small degree of interest.

She huffed.

"Whatever *is* troubling you, Alice?" her aunt Cora, The

Countess of Dunmore, inquired impatiently from the armchair opposite her. "You're huffing and puffing like a steam train." Her hazel eyes were sharp beneath her dark brows as she adjusted the pile of hair on the top of her head with an elegance that made even such a simple action seem like a statement of grace. Everything Alice's mother's sister did was beautifully orchestrated.

"Am I becoming the laughing stock of society, Aunt Cora?" Alice asked, dropping the gossip sheet on the table and picking up her teacup. It made a slight squeaking sound as she traced the rim with her forefinger. She winced and stopped immediately.

"Ah, so you have read the latest *The Society Page,* have you?" Aunt Cora asked.

Alice sighed and nodded slowly as she took a sip of tepid tea.

"Alice. Your husband's a nincompoop. You know that. I know that. Everyone who knows you knows that." She paused, then added, "in fact, everyone who knows him knows that." She closed her book and waved a hand at her niece. "So does it really matter what *The Society Page* says?"

"But Lilly? Really? She's so…so…*country.*"

She and Lilian had never been especially close, but when her younger cousin had married and come to reside on a small estate not three miles from Manning Hall, Alice had tried to make Lilly feel welcome, but the truth was they had very little in common. Like Vance, Alice's husband of fourteen years, Lilly was very much of the hunting, fishing, and shooting brigade. In contrast, Alice couldn't bear the noise of guns and barking dogs and hated the thought of ruining a beautiful pair of shoes trudging through mud and water in the name of sport. And now, according to the broadsheet, Lilly had thrown off her mourning gown (and not just metaphorically if *The Society Page* was to be believed) and returned to local society, where she'd no doubt waggled her very ample bosom in Vance's direction, and he'd welcomed her with open arms.

Alice huffed again.

"Really, Alice, enough of this!" Aunt Cora scolded. "You knew when you married Vance that you had nothing in common. I told you at the time you…"

Of course, Aunt Cora had been right. Even at the tender age of eighteen, Alice had known what she'd been getting into when she'd married the then thirty-year-old heir to the Stortford title and lands. Having returned to London society a year after his first wife's death, he'd been the catch of the season. Alice had been debutante of the year. They'd been the perfect match.

Of course, it had been well known that he'd wanted a son, something his wife had died trying to give him. Alice, being the daughter of a duke, had wanted the status and wealth she'd been used to. They should have been an ideal fit. Except Vance had been, and still was, as Aunt Cora had so rightly pointed out, a nincompoop. But with his wealth and social status, the then-young Alice had thought she could have the life she wanted. It had seemed enough then, and she'd truly thought she could make it work.

However, in reality, their wants and needs were very different. Vance liked to be in the country among his prize hunters, his precious hounds, and his loaded guns. Alice preferred town—where the most dangerous animals wore top hats and a well-placed eyebrow could be more effective than a bullet. Vance wanted to be on a horse galloping across the fields. She wanted to be shopping for shoes. He wanted to be drinking ale with his steward, discussing culling the estate's deer population. She wanted to be attending candlelit supper parties and listening to traded secrets across theatre boxes.

The only thing Vance and Alice had ever had in common were their children. Two boys. An heir and a spare. Harry and Freddie. Or to give them their full titles — Harold, Lord Treeble (aged thirteen) and Lord Frederick Manning (aged twelve). They were both at boarding school at their father's alma mater in Derbyshire. Alice missed them dreadfully and looked forward to their weekly letters. She knew they would much rather be playing rugby and cricket (Harry) or rowing and fencing (Freddie) than writing to her. But what was no doubt a chore to them was a lifeline to her.

"…so it's inevitable he'll find someone to warm his bed. Men have needs, Alice. Everyone understands that," Aunt Cora finished with a sharp nod.

Yes, I know! It was hardly unusual that once the procreation aspect of the relationship had been taken care of, a couple had to survive the next forty-odd years together. So was it really fair to expect either party to live the rest of their lives without love? Or, in her husband's case, lust?

When she'd first decamped to Darby House, she'd frequently asked herself if she should've endeavoured to make a success of it with her husband, but as time had gone on, and she'd settled into the London social scene, she'd paid little heed to the disquiet in her marriage. After all, Vance was a good father and a reasonably generous husband. *He could be so much worse.*

But, returning to the report in *The Society Page*, one thing she *had* expected from him was to be discreet about his amorous relationships. It was an unspoken agreement between them. And, until now, he'd kept his dalliances quiet. She stifled a sigh. She would need to write to her not-so-beloved and remind him of his responsibility to keep his affairs of the heart in the bedroom where they belonged, for her sake and the sake of his sons.

"Now what you need is a diversion, Alice. An interest, something like—"

Alice held her hand up and cut her aunt off. "Embroidery or painting will not suffice enough to give me a purpose, Aunt Cora," she replied firmly. "I need to do something that will make me feel useful."

She sighed again, earning a look from her aunt as she plucked up *The Society Page* off the table and turned it over, hoping for something juicy to occupy her mind.

Oh, this looks promising, she thought as she read the headline: *An Heir Apparent—or Not at All?* She read on…

The recent passing of the late Earl of Rivershore has left his household in a most delicate state of uncertainty as whispers circulate regarding the potential appearance of a hitherto absent heir.

The Dowager Countess of Rivershore, presently in residence at Rivershore Hall, is said to be conducting herself with composure, though it is widely supposed that she is not without private anxieties. Should a legitimate heir lay claim to the title and entailed estate before the prescribed legal deadline, the Countess may find herself obliged to withdraw from the home she has long presided over.

Meanwhile, her son by a former marriage, Mr Henry Somerset, has been overheard at White's Club voicing no small degree of frustration. Having managed the Rivershore estate these past three years on behalf of his late stepfather, Mr Somerset is reportedly unwilling to relinquish such responsibility without contest. Indeed, those privy to the conversation suggest he has not ruled out a legal challenge to the entail should an heir make himself known.

The matter must be resolved post-haste as the statutory deadline is understood to expire by week's end. Until then, Society watches and speculates—as is it's wont.

Henry Somerset? Hadn't she met him before? If she remembered correctly, her younger brother, James, had introduced the dashing gentleman to her. *Oh, yes, I remember him now… Altogether he's too handsome for his own good…*

Her thoughts were interrupted by the scrape of the front door being opened. There was a muffled conversation, then footsteps coming her way heralded the arrival of a letter, borne by the steady hands of Pratt, her butler. Alice immediately recognised her sister-in-law's elegant script, igniting a spark of curiosity in her otherwise dull afternoon. "It's from Fee," she told Aunt Cora.

The seal popped as she broke it. The words danced before her, filled with the vigour only Fiona, the Countess of Tilling, could inspire through mere ink and paper. She cleared her throat and read it out loud.

"My dearest Alice,

This tiresome weather must surely be dragging you down into a state of ennui. But take heart! I'm sending you a distraction—one I trust you shall not find entirely dull.

He comes in the form of The Right Honourable Lester Fairfax, brother-in-law to the late Earl of Rivershore's younger brother (though I confess I can never quite keep the Rivershore lineage straight). He finds himself in need of a certain kind of assistance, and naturally, you sprang to mind.

After the deft way in which you managed Cousin Lucy's delicate situation—"

Aunt Cora cleared her throat. Lucy's 'delicate situation' and Alice's part in covering it up was a subject her aunt treated with the same horror she reserved for bad sherry or bare ankles.

Alice carried on.

"and with so little fuss!—I assured him you would be the very person to consult. Love to Aunt Cora. Fee."

"So Lester Fairfax is back, is he?" Cora asked, leaning forward, her interest clearly piqued. "I remember him from my first season. It was before his sister had married the Earl of Rivershore's younger brother." Aunt Cora then shook her head. "Later, I remember someone telling me he'd left London with his sister and her husband. They ventured to India for tea trading, I believe," Cora mused, clearly rifling through her mental index cards of society connections.

Well, this could prove interesting. Does his problem concern the earl's heir I have just been reading about in The Society Page? I hope so! Aunt Cora was right. A diversion—and perhaps a challenge—was precisely what she needed right now.

2

AN HOUR LATER…

Alice swept into the drawing room at Darby House, the rustle of her skirts barely audible over the beating of her heart. With a quick nod, she motioned for George, her lead footman, to linger by the door—his towering frame an unspoken bastion of propriety.

There was a crackle as her guest shifted uncomfortably in his seat. He'd been sitting upright, his hands resting on top of the polished wooden cane in front of him. He rose abruptly when he saw her. "Your Grace, I'm most grateful for this audience," he boomed in a deep voice. "The Right Honourable Lester Fairfax at your service." He clicked his heels together and gave a deep bow.

Alice waved a hand at him. "Please sit down, Mr Fairfax, and tell me how I may be of help to you." She settled into the armchair opposite him, her curiosity piqued.

He glanced towards George, a frown creasing his forehead. "This matter is… er, rather private, Your Grace."

"Oh, don't mind George." She raised an eyebrow at the footman, whose blue eyes betrayed no emotion. "He's as silent as a graveyard and twice as discreet. Please proceed."

Fairfax swallowed and nodded, though his moustache twitched in what might have been annoyance or nerves. He cleared his throat, clearly steeling himself to spill the beans. "It concerns my nephew, Mr Charlie Rydal. He stands to inherit the title held by his late uncle, The Earl of River-shore." His voice carried an edge of pride that seemed at odds with his concerned expression.

Ah, so the earl's heir has turned up. And just in time, it would appear. If the newspapers were to be believed, the deadline for Mr Charlie Rydal to present himself to the earl's lawyers was the end of this week. "Well, he appears to have cut it a bit fine, Mr Fairfax, but—"

"We had to come from India, Your Grace. He's my sister's son. We manage a tea plantation out there. But now, with the earl's passing…" He trailed off, his green eyes darkening with worry.

"And your brother-in-law is here with you?"

"Alas, no. He died six months ago." Fairfax bowed his head. "And my sister is too frail to travel. So it fell upon me to escort young Charlie to London." Fairfax's hands tightened around the head of his cane, his knuckles whitening as he shifted in his seat, the leather creaking under his weight. "We arrived on Friday, and I took two rooms at The Carlton Hotel here in Mayfair. I had to depart for business in South—" He stopped and coughed. "Er… Portsmouth on Saturday after-noon…" He trailed off and cleared his throat as he rested his cane against one knee and unfolded a neatly pressed handker-chief. He dabbed at his brow, then continued, "Upon my return on Sunday evening…" His voice tapered off again, and he cast a troubled glance towards the window. "Charlie was not in his room, Your Grace, and he's still missing."

Missing? So that's what this is about? She was disap-pointed in Fee. She'd hoped for more than an errant young man who would no doubt turn up in the next few hours slightly the worse for wear and probably very sheepish. Young Rydal had discovered the bright lights of the city and was no doubt making the most of his freedom. She stifled a sigh. This wasn't the exciting puzzle she'd been expecting. "How old is your nephew, Mr Fairfax?"

"Twenty-two, Your Grace."

So an adult. "And how was he when you last saw him?"

"He was tired but in good spirits when I left."

"Well, London has its allure," Alice said with a small smile, remembering her younger brother's first weekend in London after he'd come down from Cambridge. Following an afternoon of drinking at Whites and an evening of baccarat at Brooke's, James had been unceremoniously delivered to her doorstep by an unhappy hansom cab driver the following evening with absolutely no recollection of where he'd been for the previous twenty-four hours.

"Indeed, it does." He folded his handkerchief with precise corners. "But I'm worried. Charlie has never been to London before, and he knows no one here."

"But surely the young man is simply enjoying the Capital's charms," she replied, brushing a loose strand of red hair from her face. She suppressed a yawn as the muffled Westminster chimes from the grandfather clock in the hall marked the quarter-hour. A low rumble from her stomach told her it was twelve-fifteen. *Luncheon will be ready soon.*

"Ah, Your Grace, if only it were so." Fairfax leaned forward, the concern in his green eyes deepening. "I have made a few discreet enquires myself, and no one has seen Charlie. It is unlike him to be out of contact for this long."

"Perhaps he's simply lost track of time?" She was itching to stand up and be rid of this man.

Fairfax shook his head, his scruffy moustache bristling

with resolve. "Time, dear lady, is precisely what we lack. The appointment Charlie has to attend in order to claim his inheritance is this Friday at noon. Should Charlie fail to appear…" He huffed loudly. "Well, he'll lose everything."

Alice studied Fairfax's face. His tanned skin gave him a healthy glow, but it was clear from the lines on his forehead and the worry in his eyes that he was concerned for his nephew. *But why? Friday is four days away.* She shifted to the edge of her seat. "What do you think has happened to your nephew?" she asked, her voice steady despite the unease that was knotting in her stomach.

Fairfax gave a sharp tug at his collar — a starched piece that looked like it might throttle him if given the opportunity. "Your Grace," he said, his words clipped with urgency. "I fear someone has taken him."

"Taken?" Her brow arched in surprise. "Surely, that is a rather dramatic conclusion to draw?"

He quickly glanced at George, who stood as still as one of the marble busts lining the foyer of Darby House, then back at her, lowering his voice. "But consider the timing. The inheritance—"

Was he seriously suggesting that someone had kidnapped Charlie Rydal to stop him from making the meeting on Friday and claiming his inheritance? It sounded like one of the mystery novels by Wilkie Collins that her aunt Cora had taken a shine to recently. However, she couldn't deny it was a more exciting prospect than him having lost his way home after a night of overindulgence.

"There are those who it would suit a great deal if my nephew failed to make that appointment," Fairfax continued. His eyes met hers with an intensity that bordered on pleading. "You understand the stakes, Your Grace. Please, will you help me find out what has happened to him?"

3

A FEW MINUTES LATER...

The air was heavy with the scent of beeswax and desperation as Pratt arrived in the drawing room with tea. Lester Fairfax's plea for Alice's help lingered like a fog, his eyes imploring her from across the table as the butler laid out the tea things. Alice rose and poured them both a cup, then returned to her seat opposite him. Her fingers toyed with the edge of her teacup, the porcelain cool against her fingertips. "Mr Fairfax," she said. "Your concern for your nephew is... touching." She paused. There was something about Fairfax's manner that made her feel uneasy. Did she really want to get entangled in this troublesome affair? "But I'm not sure there is much I can do that you cannot do for yourself."

She leaned back against the velvet upholstery of the armchair she was sitting in. "Why not hire a private investigator, Mr Fairfax? Surely, they're more suited to such tasks than a lady of my... social standing." She took a sip of tea as she met his gaze.

Lester Fairfax shifted uncomfortably, his hands clasped tightly around his tea cup. "The truth is, I'm somewhat of a stranger in this city now. I left twenty years ago. My contacts are... outdated at best." He glanced away as he placed his cup on the table. "And discretion is paramount. I cannot have it known that Charlie is missing. It could cause quite the scandal." He shifted, picking up his cane, which had been propped up beside him. He rested his hands on the tip of the stick. "As I said before, Your Grace, there are those who would benefit greatly from Charlie's prolonged absence."

"Indeed." Alice arched a brow, intrigued despite her reservations. "And whom do you suspect harbours such ill intent?"

"The entail is quite specific," he stated, the words clipped with urgency. "Should no legitimate heir present himself by the deadline, the title and estate default to Mr Henry Somerset, the son of the late earl's wife."

Ah, now we come to the dashing stepson... Alice could practically see him: brooding expression, chiselled jaw, those dark-brown eyes full of some noble torment. Her heart gave the faintest skip—though she chose, quite sensibly, to blame the tea.

Fairfax's cane tapped an anxious rhythm on the Persian rug.

Tap. Tap. Tap.

She wrinkled her brow. The noise amplified and filled her head. *Please stop...*

Tap. Tap. Tap.

She fluttered her fingers along her lips. *Stop, now...*

Tap. Tap. Tap

Stop! She cleared her throat loudly.

He stopped.

Alice clenched her jaw, then slowly relaxed her muscles. *And breathe...*

She stared at him. Beads of moisture glistened on his forehead. *Why is he so nervous?* And why did she get the feeling he wasn't telling her everything? She took another sip of tea.

He continued, "And with Lady Rivershore—his mother—they stand to gain everything. It is not difficult to imagine they might wish to, ah… secure such an outcome by their own means."

Alice let the suggestion hang in the air, watching as he tilted his head, his moustache twitching like the whiskers of a cornered rat.

Was he really suggesting that the Countess of Rivershore and her son would somehow harm Charlie Rydal in order to retain the late earl's estate? About to dismiss Fairfax's suggestion as farfetched, she hesitated. It was true—Lady Rivershore had a lot to lose. And although one had to hope the earl had made some provision for her in his will, if she was required to leave her homes in London, Essex, and Scotland, then that would be a substantial comedown for her.

And then there was her son, Henry Somerset. He'd been managing the earl's estates for the last few years according to *The Society Page*. He would have an expectation that he deserved to now be master, having put so much work into maintaining the family's wealth.

She frowned as she put her empty teacup down on the table between them. Why had the earl handed over the estate management to his stepson if he'd known he had a nephew who would inherit? Unless, of course, he hadn't known he'd had a nephew…

"How long ago did you and your sister's family leave England for India?" she asked.

"Twenty years ago."

So Charlie would have been two. Well, that dashed that theory.

"And did the earl and Charlie's father have much contact since you all departed?"

Fairfax's mouth fell open slightly, then he raised his hand to his mouth and cleared his throat. "Er, no." His pitch had altered, and he looked away.

Had she touched a nerve? "And why is that, Mr Fairfax?"

He coloured slightly underneath his tan. "The earl didn't approve of his brother, my sister, and myself going off to seek our fortune on another continent." He hesitated, then explained, "My own brother—I'm a younger son of an earl too—wanted me to take holy orders and, subsequently, a living at his estate in Essex. The earl wanted Charlie's father to join the navy." He gave a shrug. "Let's just say neither of us felt we were well-suited to those professions, so I persuaded my sister and her husband to come with me to India."

So was that the cause of his discomfort? The earl must have been fairly upset with Fairfax when he'd taken his sister and the earl's brother away to the other side of the world. Had he cast his brother out of his life, never expecting to hear from him again?

"And they had no further contact?"

"Quite so," he said grimly.

Alice took a deep breath. *Should I do this or not?*

As if sensing her reluctance, Fairfax shifted in his seat. "Lady Tilling spoke highly of your abilities to navigate delicate matters, Your Grace." He paused, his eyes meeting hers with calculated admiration.

"Flattery, Mr Fairfax?" She arched an eyebrow.

He gave a sly smile.

An icy shiver ran up Alice's spine. She wasn't sure she

liked this man, but she pondered his words nonetheless, weighing them against the monotony of her present daily routine. The prospect of untangling this mystery was undeniably appealing. After all, what harm could come from indulging in a little investigation?

"Very well, Mr Fairfax," she said, standing and smoothing the front of her gown. "I will see what I can find out."

"You have my utmost gratitude, Your Grace." His relief was palpable as he jumped up.

"However, let us be clear," she continued, fixing him with a steady gaze. "I make no promises. Do you understand?"

"Of course, Your Grace," he said, bowing deeply.

As the door clicked shut behind Fairfax, George began clearing up the tea things. His bulking frame filled the space, not unlike that of his father, Stokes, the butler at Francis Court, her family home.

"So, George, what do you make of Mr Fairfax's tale?" she asked him.

He straightened up, the loaded tray balanced expertly on one hand. "I believe he's concealing something, Your Grace." His voice was steady, his gaze direct. "Begging your pardon, ma'am, but there's something about him… well… not quite above-board."

She bowed her head. She trusted George's instincts, and they were seemingly aligned with her own.

"Well then, let's see if we cannot get to the bottom of Mr Fairfax and his vanishing nephew, shall we, George? I rather suspect there's more to this than meets the eye."

"Yes, ma'am." A ghost of a smile crossed his features as he bowed his head.

Alice straightened. *Well I best get on with it then.* "Please fetch Mr Beaumont for me. Tell him it is urgent."

"Right away, ma'am" He gave a curt nod, then purposely strode from the room, with the tea tray held aloft.

Left alone, she allowed herself a small, self-satisfied smile. There was a mystery to be solved, and she meant to get to the bottom of it…

5:15 PM THE SAME DAY…

The *rat-a-tat-tat* of the tradesman's door knocker in the courtyard below the window of the library caused Alice to pause in her scrutiny of *The Society Page's* back issues. Her fingers tingled. *Is that Ben Beaumont already?*

She smiled slowly as she remembered their first encounter six months earlier. The circumstances had been rather unusual.

Beaumont had been hired by the then-mistress of Alice's husband—a woman with delusions of grandeur, who had set him on Alice's trail, hoping to uncover a scandal so she could replace her as Vance's wife. Unfortunately for her, no dirt had been forthcoming, and her scheme had collapsed under the weight of its own wishful thinking.

"Your husband's romantic entanglement was less than satisfied with my report," Beaumont had told Alice back then, the first time he'd sat across from her in this very library. "She didn't care for the truth and declined to settle my fee. I feel it is only fair you should be apprised of her intent, Your Grace."

"The duke would never seek a divorce," she'd assured

him, although she'd resented being entangled in Vance's indiscretions. The woman in question had been discreetly cut adrift not long after, following one of Alice's more spirited conversations with her husband.

"I will settle your fee, Mr Beaumont. You've more than earned it," she'd said.

"Thank you for the offer, Your Grace, but I cannot accept payment from you," he'd replied and, in doing so, had won her respect. He'd secured her ongoing patronage not long after, when he'd proven himself invaluable during her cousin Lucy's recent difficulties.

The basement door creaked open, and a soft, almost inaudible exchange of words took place. The door's old hinges emitted a groan, and the door closed.

Alice shuffled the broadsheets back into a pile and turned the top one over. She moved her fountain pen aside and glanced down at her notes. Her scant research so far had revealed little in the way of gossip about either Lady River-shore or her son, Henry Somerset, except for the endless speculation of when Mr Somerset would marry and, if so, who the lucky young lady would be.

One thing had struck her though. *The Society Page,* along with the whole of London high society, had, until recently at least, assumed that Henry was his stepfather's heir. Either the countess and her son had kept the entail quiet so as not to damage Henry's marriage prospects, or it had only come to light when the earl had died. If the latter, then it must have been a tremendous blow to them both.

The muffled thud of the baize door that led from the basement opening was followed by the rhythmic footfalls of two men—presumably Mr Beaumont and either George or Pratt—as they strode across the marble flooring of the foyer. The ringing quality to their steps changed as they moved onto the carpet runner in the corridor leading towards her, the faint creaks of the wooden floorboards beneath the carpet now punctuating their strides.

Alice rose from the desk and moved to stand in front of it. The library door opened with a *swish,* and the two men stepped in.

"Mr Beaumont to see you, Your Grace," George said, ushering in the private investigator with the quiet deference he extended to those he trusted.

"Thank you, George," Alice replied with a nod. Beaumont removed his bowler hat, revealing small streaks of grey amidst his brown hair.

"Good afternoon, Your Grace," he greeted, his sharp blue eyes scanning the room before resting on her. A scar, a souvenir from some long ago altercation, accentuated his rugged features.

"Mr Beaumont." She greeted him with a faint smile. "Thank you for coming on such short notice. Do sit down. May I offer you tea—or perhaps something a touch stronger?"

The private investigator glanced briefly at his watch, then nodded. "A whisky wouldn't go amiss, Your Grace."

She turned to George, who was waiting quietly by the door. "And I shall take a small sherry, thank you, George."

The footman bowed and departed.

"Is he still in your confidence, Your Grace?" Beaumont asked as soon as the door was closed.

She nodded. "He is, and I trust him completely. Feel free to talk to him about this case if you wish to."

"I will," the investigator remarked casually, yet she detected an underlying note of approval. "Trust is a rare commodity these days. You're fortunate to have it within your household."

She dipped her head. He was right, of course. With society's insatiable desire for gossip and titbits, she was lucky that nothing had ever leaked from Darby House. Well, nothing that she hadn't already pre-approved, of course.

A creak from the door as it was pushed fully open heralded George's return with their beverages, and Alice invited Beaumont to take a seat on the sofa while she made herself comfortable in an armchair opposite him. As George handed out the drinks and retired to the back of the room, she told Beaumont about the visit from Lester Fairfax and recounted his story about the disappearance of his nephew. Throughout, Beaumont listened intently, dipping his head occasionally. He took no notes as usual, but she'd yet to witness him unable to recall all the pertinent facts in a case.

"A missing heir, eh? I like the sound of that, Your Grace," Ben said when she finished. "To start with, a visit to The Carlton Hotel is required. I would like to know more about when this Charlie Rydal left and who might've been with him. Let's see if we can verify Fairfax's account of events." He rose smoothly to his feet. "I shall uncover what I can and report back posthaste."

Alice stood too. "Thank you, Mr Beaumont. Your discretion is, as always, invaluable."

"Discretion is my middle name, Your Grace," he said with a wry smile, tipping his hat as he turned and, with a swift, purposeful stride, left the room.

***

"Arms up, if you please, Your Grace," Maud, Alice's maid, instructed, her slender fingers deftly working the laces of

Alice's corset. The maid's chestnut curls, always pinned away from her thoughtful eyes, bobbed with each precise movement. She was patient and firm, the most desirable attributes of a lady's maid.

Alice's bedchamber was awash with the muted glow coming from the gas sconces. The walls, dressed in a damask paper of cream and rose, held the day's last light captive, while outside, dusk settled over Mayfair like a velvet shawl. She complied with a lift of her arms. "What would I do without you, Maud?"

"Stumble into dinner in your dressing gown, I shouldn't wonder, ma'am," Maud said, her lips curling in a knowing smile.

"Quite right," Alice said with a soft chuckle. "A scandal worthy of the gossip columns." *Talking of scandals*... "Maud, do you know anyone in the employ of the recently widowed Countess of Rivershore?" Her maid's vast family connections —she had seven sisters, five brothers, and eleven cousins, all in service—meant there was a fairly good chance she would.

Maud paused, her hands stilling against the silk of Alice's gown. She tilted her head slightly, her eyes keen with curiosity. "Is there something you wish to know, ma'am?"

"An enquiry of a... delicate nature," Alice replied vaguely. "One that calls for... discreet channels."

"Say no more, ma'am." Maud resumed her task with renewed purpose. "My cousin Judith's in her ladyship's employ."

"May I ask you to speak with Judith then?" Alice asked, her eyes meeting Maud's in the mirror. "See if she might share her thoughts on her employer—and how the countess and her son have fared since the earl's passing?"

"Consider it done, ma'am." Maud grinned. "If there's anything amiss, Judith will have wind of it."

Alice watched as her maid secured the final hook of her gown with practiced ease. "You're a treasure, Maud."

"I know," she replied, a grin spreading over her face.

"And so modest," Alice accused playfully as they both laughed.

***

In the drawing room of Darby House, the large velvet navy-blue curtains had been drawn, giving the room a cosy feel as the small fire merrily blazed away along the back wall, keeping away the summer chill that the wet weather had brought. George handed Alice a glass of claret as she entered, then bowed and left the room.

"Evening, Aunt Cora," she said, settling into a chair with a rustle of her silk skirts.

"Good evening, Alice," Aunt Cora replied from the plush couch opposite, a glass of sherry in her hand. She cocked her head to one side. "What are *you* so excited about?"

Alice started briefly. Clearly, she was failing to hide her interest in the curious puzzle of the missing heir. She took a sip of the deep-red wine and said nothing.

"Am I to assume you have decided to help Fairfax then?" Alice hadn't had a chance to give Aunt Cora an account of her meeting with Lester Fairfax yet as her aunt had been out for afternoon tea with a group of her old cronies. She gave her a summary of Fairfax's concerns for his nephew.

"Well, well," Aunt Cora proclaimed after Alice finished. "That's quite a tale." She took a sip of her sherry.

"Indeed." Alice paused, then asked, "Aunt Cora, you're

well acquainted with the Countess of Rivershore, are you not?"

"I am," her aunt confirmed. "Although, I've not seen her since the passing of her husband. May he rest in peace." She bowed her head dramatically.

"Then perhaps we should pay her a visit tomorrow afternoon," Alice suggested hopefully. "To express our condolences, naturally."

"Hmmm…" Aunt Cora arched a perfectly sculpted eyebrow. "And possibly observe her?"

Alice shrugged nonchalantly. "And perhaps her son too if he's at home?"

Aunt Cora hesitated for a minute, then said, "Very well. It does seem fitting to offer our sympathies in person." Her eyes held a glint of excitement.

"Thank you, aunt." A small smile curled the corners of Alice's mouth. She was content that her plans had been set into motion.

5

THE NEXT AFTERNOON...

The victoria rattled to a stop outside the imposing facade of Rivershore House in Belgravia. The metallic *clink* of the horses' harnesses and the *creak* of the seat at the front of the carriage signalled that Alice's coachman was securing the mares before jumping down to help them out. As he offered up his hand to Aunt Cora, Alice glanced out of the window at the grand, sprawling structure of the hereditary home of the Earl of Rivershore, with its massive street-facing windows and a heavy, ornate blue front door. It was much larger and more impressive than Darby House, more along the lines of her husband's London home, Stortford Place. How would Lady Rivershore feel if she lost this house—her home—to an unknown young nephew-in-law from India? Alice could only imagine how worried the countess must be at this moment.

The iron-grey London sky was at least rain-free, and as Alice took her coachman's hand and stepped out of the carriage, the gushing river of mud and horse muck that had been running alongside the pavement for days had now slowed down to more of a trickle. Glad she'd changed from her button boots with their delicate embroidered sides, into her sensible lace-up brown boots, she smoothed the folds of her gown as she joined Aunt Cora on the pavement where her aunt was straightening her hat.

"Best if I lead the conversation, I think," Aunt Cora whispered as a dour-looking butler came forward to greet them. They followed him up the steps and through the grand entrance. The interior of Rivershore House was as impressive as the exterior, with high ceilings, polished marble floors, and plush furnishings that reeked of wealth and status.

They were ushered into the drawing room, its heavy drapes making the room dark despite the bank of windows along one side of the room. The butler coughed discreetly. "Her Grace, the Duchess of Stortford, and the Countess of Dunmore, my lady," he announced in a stiff voice.

There was a rustle as Lady Rivershore, dressed in a black dress trimmed with crepe, rose from an armchair and moved towards Aunt Cora, with her arms out in front of her. "Cora. How lovely to see you! I was so pleased to get your message yesterday to say you would call." Her smooth and cultured voice had a slight tremor hinting at unease.

Has she guessed that our motive for visiting is not merely to pay our respects following her husband's recent demise?

Aunt Cora greeted her friend with equal warmth, taking her outstretched hands in hers. "My dearest Catherine. I wanted to come in person and express my condolences on Robert's passing. Such a remarkable gentleman. Kind, generous, and devoted to you and your son. His loss is no doubt deeply felt by all who had the privilege to know him."

Alice suppressed a smile. Aunt Cora was really laying it on thick. If she remembered rightly, her aunt had previously described the earl to her as, "a corpulent wind-bag full of his own consequence".

Lady Rivershore's striking blue eyes filled with tears. She whispered, "Thank you," to Aunt Cora as she dropped her hands and moved over to a small side table, where she retrieved a lace handkerchief from a porcelain holder. She dabbed her eyes, then, still holding on to it in her hand, she turned to Alice with a weak smile. "And you've brought your niece. I hope you're well, Your Grace?"

Alice politely dipped her head. "Very well, thank you, Your Ladyship. I, too, would like to add my sincerest sympathy on the loss of your husband."

Lady Rivershore dipped her chin and swiftly dabbed her eyes again.

Poor woman. She must be upset that her husband's death has left her in such a precarious position. Alice hesitated. Was she being cynical? It *was* possible that the countess had really loved him. *It happens.*

Feeling a spot of heat in her cheeks, she looked away. And that was when she saw Henry Somerset. He stood in the shadows over by the fireplace on the far side of the room. As he moved slightly out of the darkness, Alice gave an involuntarily sharp intake of breath. She'd quite forgotten how effortlessly he drew the eye—and how difficult it was to look away.

He said nothing, but his presence commanded attention nonetheless. Alice tilted her chin up—the brooding set of his brow and the slight shadow on his chiselled jawline, drawing her attention. He was one of the most striking men she'd seen. The heat in her cheeks increased. She glanced down at the floor.

"You've met my son, Mr Henry Somerset, before, no doubt?" the countess asked as she beckoned him over to where they stood. "Henry, this is my good friend the

Countess of Dunmore. And this is her niece, Her Grace, the Duchess of Stortford."

He bowed first to Aunt Cora, then turned to Alice. "I've had the pleasure," he said, his voice like velvet—smooth and rich. "I trust your brother is well, Your Grace?"

A shiver danced down Alice's spine. "He is indeed," she squeaked—then hastily cleared her throat.

"Shall we sit?" Lady Rivershore led them over to a sitting area by the windows and indicated for them to take the sofa with its back to the light. "Tea will be here soon."

With a rustle of skirts, the ladies settled themselves down. From the corner of her eye, Alice watched Henry Somerset stride back to the fireplace, where the darkness swallowed him up once again.

"We're in such a state of limbo, Cora, waiting for news of Robert's heir." The countess wasted no time in informing them of her woes. "No doubt you've read all about it in the… *papers*." Her face pinched as she said the word. "It's quite unbearable."

Aunt Cora nodded slowly. "I can imagine. So he's not appeared yet then?"

Lady Rivershore shook her head as she lifted her handkerchief to her nose.

"And have you ever met him?"

"Once, perhaps. Not long after I married Robert," she replied, waving her empty hand. "Charlie would've only been a few years old. Then came the smallpox, poor child." She shook her head sadly.

Charlie had smallpox? That's serious. He's lucky to still be alive…

"They left for India shortly after that, and we heard nothing more," Lady Rivershore continued. "We assumed the child had died either during the crossing or not long after they arrived."

Assumed? Past tense... Alice's eyebrow quirked instinctively. *That implies she now knows otherwise...* "But he'd not?"

The countess hesitated, then gave a brittle laugh. "He was sickly and weak." She glanced over at her son, but it was too dark to see his reaction. "So, yes, of course he died," she added, sounding somewhat flustered. "But the lawyers say they must follow the right procedure, so we just have to be patient..." She trailed off as she slumped back in her armchair with an exasperated sigh.

Did she just admit, then try to cover up that she knows Charlie Rydal is, in fact, alive and currently in the country? The rattle of a tea tray outside stopped Alice from asking more questions. *But one thing I* am *sure of is that she is hiding something.*

***

Alice sipped her drink, trying hard not to drop the elegant and fragile porcelain cup, whose narrow, dainty handle she was holding on to for dear life. *Why do they make them so small?* Aware that Henry was sitting opposite her, having joined them to take tea, she quickly returned her cup to its saucer with a gentle *clink*.

"Henry has been studying estate management under his stepfather's guidance, you know," Lady Rivershore shared, breaking the silence of the last five minutes.

"Indeed," Aunt Cora responded, returning her plate to the table in front of her, now devoid of the generous slice of

Victoria sponge she'd just devoured. "I'm surprised Robert would invest so much time in preparing Mr Somerset when he knew someone else would inherit the estate."

Henry, who had remained silent since their earlier introduction, finally spoke. "My stepfather was a pragmatic man. He knew there was no surviving heir."

His steady delivery and firm tone gave what he said an air of sincerity. *Have I got it wrong?* Was there a chance that they *didn't* know Charlie Rydal was here, after all? And yet… She glanced at Aunt Cora. Her aunt wasn't giving anything away. After a few seconds, she rose, and they bid a brief farewell, mindful not to outstay their welcome.

They followed the butler out of the room but had barely taken two steps into the hallway before Aunt Cora paused to adjust her gloves and smooth her skirts. Alice, momentarily ahead of her, turned to offer assistance—and in doing so, her gaze drifted toward the drawing room where the heavy double doors remained slightly ajar.

She hesitated.

Through the narrow opening, she could just make out the figures of Lady Rivershore and her son, their heads close together. They were speaking in low voices, but the acoustics of the old house muffled the words entirely. She narrowed her eyes and concentrated on their lips.

"He's not going anywhere until I say so." Henry's face was tight with frustration.

Alice froze, a chill crawling across her skin. *Who's not going anywhere?*

Lady Rivershore stepped closer, wringing a lace-edged handkerchief in her pale hands. Her mouth formed a whisper. "What if someone finds out?"

Henry gave a dismissive flick of his hand. "Then we deny everything."

Alice's pulse kicked. *Heavens above! Are they talking about Charlie Rydal?*

Wait…they could be talking about anything.

Harumph! The butler cleared his throat. Alice took an instinctive step back just as she felt Aunt Cora's hand touch her elbow.

"All right, my dear?" her aunt asked.

"Yes," Alice replied automatically, though her mind was already spinning. *Did I just witness a confession?*

On the cobbled street outside, the bustling noise of city life filled the air as they waited for their carriage. The distant *clip-clop* of horses' hooves suggested it wouldn't be long. Her mind replaying what she's just witnessed, Alice turned to her aunt. "What do you make of it, Aunt Cora?"

Aunt Cora met Alice's gaze, her hazel eyes sharp. "Catherine's hiding something, I fear. Robert was a pompous bore. I cannot imagine Catherine cared much for him, yet she seems truly upset. Something is afoot."

Alice's heart sunk. "Do you suppose they could have… well, *done* something to Charlie?" she asked, concern lacing her words.

Aunt Cora pressed her lips tight and looked away for a moment. Then she turned back, her expression sombre. "I fervently hope not, my dear."

***

"Mr Beaumont, Your Grace." George stood to one side as the smartly dressed investigator strolled into the library.

"Good afternoon, Your Grace." He stopped and bowed.

Alice rose slowly from behind the desk. Her limbs felt

like lead, and her head was fuzzy. She took a deep breath and forced herself to smile. "Good afternoon, Mr Beaumont. Would you like a drink?"

He glanced at his watch, then shook his head. "Not until after five o'clock, Your Grace." He offered no further explanation of this self-imposed rule, so she gestured for him to take a seat on a sofa close to the window. George remained by the door.

"I have news," Ben said as he sat down and rested his hat next to him on the couch.

She took the chair opposite. *Already?* She was impressed.

"Saturday afternoon, there was a sighting at the hotel. A woman, Your Grace. She asked to speak to Mr Fairfax."

Did she now? "What do we know about this woman?"

"She gave her name to the clerk at the front desk as Mrs Judith Willis."

Alice frowned, trying to clear the fog in her brain. *Now that name sounds familiar… um… Ah, yes!* Willis was Maud's surname. And hadn't she told her that her cousin was called Judith? "I believe it may have been Lady Rivershore's maid."

He arched an eyebrow.

"Did the clerk give you a description?" She could then ask Maud if it matched that of Judith.

He dipped his head. "He said she had a regal air about her. Slender and elegant, with dark hair, high cheekbones, and large blue eyes."

Now that sounds very familiar. Her mouth slackened. *Could it be?* "That sounds like Lady Rivershore."

The private investigator tilted his head. "She could've been using her maid's name as a disguise, Your Grace."

"So did she meet with him?" Alice held her breath, fearing she already knew the answer.

Ben pulled a face. "Fairfax was not there. He'd already left for Portsmouth. However, the clerk contacted Charlie Rydal in his room, and not long after that, he came down, then him and the lady went into one of the guest-only sitting rooms."

She exhaled. So they'd spoken! *The countess had lied.* "How long did she stay? And did they leave together?"

"Only about ten minutes, according to the clerk, then the lady left. He said she looked rather flustered."

"And Mr Rydal?"

"The clerk saw him go back up the stairs after she'd departed."

So he'd been alive when she'd left. That was something, at least.

"Excellent work, Mr Beaumont. My aunt and I visited Lady Rivershore and her son only this afternoon. She informed us that the heir was dead. So either she was lying" —Alice's eyes narrowed slightly—"or she left the hotel and returned later to murder him."

"Er," Ben spluttered. "That may be something of a stretch, Your Grace."

Spoilsport! "Yes, you may be right," she said. "But she's clearly not to be trusted."

"On that point, I shall gladly agree."

So what to do next? Her head was a mass of cotton wool. She looked down at the boots poking out from the bottom of her skirts. A rich deep-blue in a supple leather. She wiggled her toes. So comfortable. *Blue... The sea. The ship.* Hadn't Fairfax said that his nephew knew no one here? *But is that likely?*

Alice recalled an uncle on her father's side who had recently returned from a journey to North America aboard the White Star Line. Over dinner at Francis Court, he'd spoken of all the connections he'd made during the crossing—even renewing an old school acquaintance. Was it truly possible that Fairfax and his nephew had formed no such associations during their long voyage from India?

"Mr Beaumont," she said thoughtfully. "Might you discover which vessel brought Mr Fairfax and Mr Rydal to England? I believe they docked on Friday. And, if possible, could you obtain a copy of the passenger list?"

"Of course, Your Grace. May I ask—what's your thinking?"

"I shall continue my efforts to learn why Lady Rivershore was less than truthful," Alice replied. "But it occurs to me that Mr Rydal may well have made one or more acquaintances during the voyage. Perhaps someone in whom he confided—or someone he encountered without his uncle's knowledge."

Beaumont gave a brisk nod. "A sound line of inquiry." He took up his hat and rose. "I shall attend to it without delay, Your Grace. I'll also go back to the hotel and talk to the staff who were working later on Saturday to see if they saw Mr Rydal leave."

She stood too. "Thank you, Mr Beaumont."

He made for the door, but as George stepped forward to open it, Beaumont paused, his hat only inches from his head. "Er—there's one other thing, Your Grace."

He turned back, a puzzled expression crossing his face as he slowly lowered the hand holding his bowler. "It's been bothering me since I left the hotel."

Alice tilted her head, inviting him to continue.

"I noticed a boy lingering outside. He was there when I went in and still there when I came out. Not conspicuously, mind you—but it's my business to notice such things."

He hesitated. "I recognised him. He is one of—" He

stopped himself, then added, "It's of no consequence, perhaps, but I did wonder if he was keeping watch. And whether it might be connected to Mr Rydal's disappearance." Beaumont rubbed the scar on his left cheek, his brow furrowed as he slowly shook his head.

Alice's stomach fluttered. *Could this boy be in the employ of Lady Rivershore? Or Henry Somerset?*

6

—————

THAT EVENING...

I n her bedchamber, Alice exhaled a measured breath as her maid Maud drew the corset tighter.

"Remember to breathe shallow, Your Grace," Maud said, her fingers deftly pulling at the ties.

"Is this truly necessary, Maud?" Alice asked. "You know the doctors now claim it is quite injurious to be laced so tightly. Bad for one's lungs—and digestion. Dr William Flower recently wrote—"

"Begging your pardon, ma'am, but what would a gentleman know of it?" Maud interrupted. "You're a lady of standing. You must dress accordingly."

"But it's only Aunt Cora and me this evening."

"Even so, ma'am—you must look your best," Maud replied firmly. "Her ladyship will expect no less."

"Yes, well, I should also like to breathe," Alice muttered, her voice slightly strained as Maud gave another brisk tug. She caught her reflection in the looking glass before her. The corset, she admitted, did wonders for her figure. Still— "I rather prefer breathing to swooning onto the parlour floor." She raised an eyebrow.

Maud's lips twitched with the barest hint of amusement. "Naturally, ma'am. But fashion seldom makes allowances for comfort."

I swear she enjoys this!

Maud picked up a deep-emerald gown from the chair next to them and helped Alice into it. As Maud fastened the many small fabric-covered buttons on the back, Alice's gaze returned to the mirror. The dress complemented the fiery cascade of her hair and the verdant sparkle of her green eyes. *I don't look too bad for someone who turned the grand old age of two-and-thirty nine days ago!*

"I spoke with Judith, ma'am—you recall, the one in service to Lady Rivershore," Maud said, catching Alice's gaze in the mirror.

"And?"

"She says her ladyship's a fair mistress and the household staff seem content enough..." Maud's voice trailed off as she moved to Alice's right, plucked a small key from the pocket of her apron, and bent down to unlock a drawer in the vanity unit. From it, she removed a finely crafted wooden case, elegantly inlaid with mother-of-pearl. Maud opened the lid, and from a plush red velvet compartment, she removed a necklace of perfectly round pearls strung together on a delicate silk thread.

"And Mr Henry Somerset?" Alice asked as she dipped her head forward.

"He worked closely with the earl." Maud gently laid the necklace on Alice's neck and clipped close the gold clasp. "And no one in the household knew of the entail. The staff are now fearful that a stranger will claim the earl's seat."

Alice's hand automatically went to the pearls as she raised her head and turned to face her maid. "And what of Lady

Rivershore?" *Now she knows the heir is alive, is she making plans to leave?*

"Terrified of eviction, according to Judith, but Mr Somerset has assured her they are staying where they are."

Really? That's bold... Unless...

Maud's voice lowered conspiratorially. "Judith was in the room when he told her ladyship that he had it all in hand."

Did he, indeed? Did Somerset's certainty stem from sinister deeds?

"Thank you, Maud. That's most helpful. Now—" she lifted the hem of her gown to reveal black-stockinged feet. "Let's not forget the most essential element. Shoes, if you please, Maud."

"Of course, ma'am." Maud grinned. She, too, shared her mistress' fondness for footwear, and she presented a pair of dainty green velvet slippers with a flourish.

"Ah, perfect." Alice slipped her feet into them, savouring the soft caress against her skin. "Even if I must endure this wretched contraption"—she tapped her corseted waist—"I shall be consoled by beautifully comfortable shoes."

"Very good, ma'am." Maud stepped back, surveying her handiwork with satisfaction. "You'll pass muster," she said, grinning.

***

The rustle of her skirts provided a soft cascade amidst the hush of the evening as Alice descended the stairs. As she entered the drawing room, Pratt gave a brief bow. "Good evening, Your Grace. Champagne?"

"Good evening, Pratt. Yes, please."

As the butler headed towards the sideboard along the far side of the wall, Alice walked under the grand chandelier that bathed the room in a warm, golden glow, towards the plush velvet sofas and leather armchairs that were arranged around a marble fireplace, its mantlepiece lined with family portraits in gilded frames.

Pop! Alice jumped.

"I'm so sorry, ma'am." Pratt's face was lined with concern.

"I'm fine, Pratt," Alice said as her heart rate reduced and her ears stopped ringing. She sat down on a deep-red sofa while Pratt masterfully poured her bubbling drink into a slender flute. He placed the bottle back in the ice bucket and walked towards her.

"Your drink, ma'am," he offered with a short bow as he reached her side.

"Thank you, Pratt," she replied, taking a sip, the liquid cool and fizzy against her lips.

The butler returned to his station by the door while Alice put down her drink and picked up a copy of *The Illustrated Police News*. Would the famous Sherlock Holmes be featured in any of the articles this week? She'd not seen him mentioned for a few weeks now. A tingle ran up her spine. *Perhaps he has gone undercover somewhere on a big case...*

She knew it wasn't considered appropriate for a lady of her standing to have an interest in crime, but that didn't stop her from poring over the police reports each week. She liked to study the cases, mentally collate the evidence, and come to her own judgement before finally reading the article's conclusion. Although, on occasion, the readiness of the courts to convict on what seemed to Alice to be scant proof concerned her, she was generally content that the criminal justice system was functioning adequately.

She scanned the newspaper, skim-reading for anything interesting that would catch her eye. *Two young men charged with riotous conduct outside the Adelphi Theatre... A man killed by a fourteen-pound bowling ball... A medical man who had died from drinking too much gin in Walworth. 'He used to drink a pint before breakfast,' reported a witness.* Alice's nose wrinkled. *How could someone—*

She stopped. Footsteps approached. George entered the room with a nod to Pratt, then turned to Alice. "Mr Beaumont to see you, ma'am, with another gentleman. They beg your pardon for the intrusion at such an hour but requested that they speak with you now if possible. I have shown them into the library."

Alice set down the paper and rose. Mr Beaumont must have found out something important. And another man? Her stomach fluttered. *Could it be he's located Charlie Rydal already?* "Pratt, should my aunt appear, please tell her I shall not be long." The butler bowed, and she followed George out of the room.

"George, please stay. I would like you to hear what they have to say," Alice said in a hushed voice to her lead footman as she entered The Library a few minutes later. George dipped his chin and moved to stand next to the drinks cabinet by the sideboard.

Alice stopped as abruptly as if she'd walked straight into a wall. She stifled a gasp. *Surely, that can't be...* She stared at the man looming behind Ben Beaumont. Her jaw slackened, and she fought the urge to close her eyes and shake her head.

It is *him!*

Her pulse quickened. She would recognised that hawk-like face anywhere — *Sherlock Holmes*! *In my house!*

She resisted the compulsion to giggle.

Pull yourself together, Alice! You're a duchess and should behave like one.

She rearranged her features to look as if seeing the greatest detective of all time in her library was an everyday occurrence.

"Good evening, Your Grace," Ben Beaumont greeted, tipping his hat. "May I present Mr Sherlock Holmes?"

Holmes inclined his head, a glint of curiosity in his eyes. "I'm delighted to make your acquaintance, Your Grace."

Oh my goodness! Calm, Alice. Calm..."Mr Holmes. Likewise." She smiled shyly, her voice steady despite feeling as if there wasn't enough air in the room. "I'm quite familiar with your work."

"Indeed?" Holmes arched an eyebrow.

Why did you say that? A silence hung in the air. Holmes leaned slightly forward, clearly waiting for her to expand on her comment. *Now what do I say?* Should she confess to being a devotee of *The Illustrated Police News*? Her aunt thought her interest in "riff-raffs, scallywags, and murderers" was quite macabre and had frequently pointed out that it was an unsuitable interest for a lady of the aristocracy. *Perhaps it will be best not to say anything. Yes.* She'd just carry on as if this was all perfectly normal. After all, if she was patient, Ben would surely explain why the one and only Sherlock Holmes was currently in her house, scrutinising her like she was a rare fossil.

She plastered a smile on her face, then turned her attention to Ben. "You have news?"

"Yes, Your Grace. You may well recall I told you I'd spotted a young boy watching the hotel when I was there earlier?"

Alice nodded.

"He was one of my lookouts, Your Grace," Holmes cut in before Beaumont could answer.

Holmes was having The Carlton watched? She raised an eyebrow.

"It seems we may have mutual interests. I believe from what Mr Beaumont here has told me, you're interested in Mr Charlie Rydal."

"Indeed, Mr Holmes. He's gone missing, and I have been... er asked to locate him for a concerned family member."

"Would that be Mr Lester Fairfax?"

How did he know? Her eyes narrowed as she studied his face. A smile was twitching at a corner of his mouth. *Of course. He is Sherlock Holmes. He knows everything... Well then, let us see what this is about.* "Would you gentlemen care to sit and take a drink with me while you elaborate further, Mr Holmes?"

Both men asked for brandy, which George prepared while Alice moved to the couch, and they followed, each taking an armchair on the other side of the low table in front of her. Alice gratefully took the glass of champagne George handed her. "Please continue, Mr Holmes." She took a sip of the fizzy liquid, the bubbles pinging in her mouth.

"Someone is smuggling stolen goods out of Asia, Your Grace." The light from the chandelier cast elongated shadows across his lined features. "Indian artefacts, to be precise. Many are worth a fortune, including a royal gold and diamond anklet called *The Nizam Blaze*." He took a photograph out of his pocket and passed it to her.

She looked down at the image in her hand. The anklet was composed of finely wrought metal, presumably gold, forming a delicate chain with intricate filigree and engraved floral patterns clearly visible even in the grey-scale tones of the photograph. Set into the chain were many round-cut diamonds, with larger cushion-cut diamonds prominently placed at intervals, their size and clarity making them stand out even without colour. The focal point, a teardrop-shaped diamond pendant hanging from the anklet, was surrounded by a halo of smaller stones. *It must be even more beautiful in real life,* she thought as she raised an eyebrow. *Looking at that setting. It must be worth a—*

"As you can imagine, it's of considerable value in terms of both money and history," Holmes added.

She tilted her head to one side. "And what has this got to do with the disappearance of Charlie Rydal, Mr Holmes?"

"Nothing that I know of, Your Grace."

She frowned. *Then what brings you here?*

"It's Mr Lester Fairfax I'm interested in. He exports tea from India—and it's believed he occasionally includes a few additions not declared to customs."

"Stolen artefacts, I presume?"

"Exactly so."

It seemed a little farfetched to her. After all, he was the younger son of an earl and a respectable gentleman. She plucked at the sleeve of her gown.

Holmes coughed. "Unfortunately, we've no firm evidence at the moment. Which is why I hope you can help me."

Me? Help you? Alice felt light-headed. Was Sherlock Holmes asking for *her* help?

"But first, let me share with you what my lads observed at The Carlton."

Alice had been so caught up in the case of the missing artefacts, she'd almost forgotten they were trying to find Charlie Rydal. "I would be most grateful, Mr Holmes."

"They observed Charlie Rydal departing The Carlton

Hotel at five o'clock in the evening on Saturday. He was not alone."

So *after* Lady Rivershore had visited. Had she gone back for him?

"Go on," she urged, leaning forward.

"An unidentified man joined him in a coach. My men were unable to discern his identity—"

Henry Somerset?

"—but…" Holmes paused for dramatic effect. "They recognised the crest emblazoned upon the vehicle. It belongs to the Earl of Foxworth."

"Foxworth?" Alice repeated, trying to drag something of the man from her brain but to no avail.

Ben coughed. Alice turned to him and raised an eyebrow.

"The Earl of Foxworth was named on the passenger list of the ship Charlie Rydal and his uncle arrived on," he told her.

So I was right! Charlie Rydal had made an acquaintance during his voyage. Her eyes went to the Persian rug on the floor in front of the fireplace. *Is it that simple, after all?* Had Charlie gone to spend a few days with a new friend and forgotten to tell his uncle? She would ask Ben to—

She looked up and caught Mr Holmes' gaze. *Goodness, I am being rude.* "Well, thank you, Mr Holmes. That's been very useful." She glanced over at Ben, who jerked his chin down. "So what can I do to help you in return?"

"I understand from Mr Beaumont here that you spoke with Mr Lester Fairfax yesterday, Your Grace?" he asked, his eyes sharp and assessing.

"That's correct." Alice's fingers lightly grazed the pearls around her neck.

"Would you be kind enough to recount your conversation with him, please? I'm especially interested in anything he said about his own movements since docking here on Friday."

Alice took a sip of champagne and gave him a summary of her conversation with Fairfax.

"He had business in Portsmouth, you say?" Holmes asked after she'd finished. He appeared disappointed.

A discreet cough came from the back of the room. Alice turned to meet George's eyes. "Yes, George?"

"I beg your pardon, ma'am, but I believe Mr Fairfax, in fact, went to Southampton on business, not Portsmouth. You may recall he began to say the word Southampton, then covered it up by saying Portsmouth."

She frowned. *Good heavens. I think he's right.* She smiled at George before turning back to Sherlock Holmes. "I do believe George is correct, Mr Holmes."

"Southampton! Ah, that's better…" A flicker of intrigue crossed his face, and he dipped his chin. "Yes, that's most pertinent indeed." He rose. "Well, thank you, Your Grace. I will take my leave now. I'm glad we could be of some assistance to each other."

Had she been any help? If so, he clearly wasn't going to elaborate. Alice stood and gave him a curt nod. "I'm glad to be of service, Mr. Holmes."

He gave a short bow in return. "If you need me at any time, Your Grace, I can be found at 221B Baker Street."

Alice tapped a finger against her lips as the door clicked shut behind Sherlock Holmes. She let out a *whoosh* of breath, then turned to Ben. "Well, that was unexpected, Mr Beaumont."

"Indeed, Your Grace. It would seem that young Mr Rydal has gone off somewhere in the Earl of Foxworth's carriage and not returned."

"No, I meant—" She stopped. Beaumont didn't need to

know that her heart was still racing from having had the famous detective in her house. *Get your mind back on the case, Alice!* "Er, yes. So the question is, did he go voluntarily, or has someone kidnapped him?" She needed to determine if Somerset and Foxworth were known to each other. And if they were, then could the earl have made off with Rydal on Somerset's or Lady Rivershore's bidding?

George, his statuesque figure still standing bolt upright along the oak-panelled wall, cleared his throat.

Alice nodded.

"Ma'am, if I may be so bold, I have an acquaintance who serves the Earl of Foxworth."

Well, that's a stroke of luck.

"His butler," George continued. "We're both members of The London Servant's Club. If anyone knows the earl's whereabouts, it will be him. It's my day off tomorrow, and I'll endeavour to bump into him."

"George, you're a veritable treasure," she said, her spirits buoyed by the prospect of something useful at last. "I shall leave it with you two gentlemen to locate the Earl of Foxworth. Kindly inform me the moment you learn anything of significance." The men both bowed and withdrew.

Alice stood alone in the library. She could hardly believe that had all really happened. To think, Sherlock Holmes himself had required her assistance. Smiling to herself, she smoothed down her skirts, then hurried from the room to join her aunt.

7

LATER THAT EVENING...

"What do you know about the Earl of Foxworth, Aunt?" Alice asked when they retired to the drawing room after dinner. "Wasn't there some bother about him a few years back?"

Aunt Cora took a sip of her brandy. "Yes. He left England rather hastily a couple of years ago. An investment tumbled —spectacularly. Quite a few of the *ton* were less than pleased with his er... guidance."

That was it—Alice remembered now. He'd advised several senior members of London society to invest in a scheme he'd been promoting, and it had ended quite badly. In fact, one of Vance's uncles had been obliged to sell his estate in Ireland to recoup his losses.

"He left to let the tempers in Mayfair cool," Aunt Cora continued, a wry smile playing at the edges of her lips. "I hear he has reappeared in the past week or thereabouts, spreading some fanciful tale about a gold mine."

Alice's mind was racing ahead. She pictured Charlie Rydal, young and untested, with a soon-to-be large inheritance burning a hole in his pocket. She could imagine

Foxworth waiting until Charlie's uncle, Fairfax, was out of the way, then whisking the lad away somewhere. There he could whisper sweet promises of untold riches to the naïve Charlie until he signed on the dotted line. *I hope we're not too late!*

Aunt Cora put her glass down and stood, yawning. "Well, goodnight, my dear. I believe I shall retire now."

Lady Rivershore!

"Wait, Aunt Cora," Alice said quickly, catching her aunt's attention before she had got more than halfway across the room. "I must speak to you about Lady Rivershore. She was seen at the hotel with Charlie Rydal before he disappeared, and I'd like to ask her why."

Aunt Cora paused, her hazel eyes considering the request. "It will be difficult. Catherine's in mourning, after all."

Alice sighed. *Of course.* Lady Rivershore would be unable to accept another invitation from her or Aunt Cora given they'd already called to pay their respects. She looked hopefully at her aunt. "Is there any way around it?"

Aunt Cora leaned in and kissed Alice's cheek. "I shall send a note at first light and ask if she will receive us. Now goodnight, Alice."

"Thank you, Aunt," Alice murmured, relief softening her features. "Goodnight." With that, Aunt Cora disappeared up the grand staircase, leaving Alice alone with her thoughts. *I need a port and some peace and quiet...*

***

Alice swirled the deep-ruby liquid in her glass, the rich aroma mingling with the scent of polished wood that pervaded the library. Footsteps approached, and Pratt appeared at the threshold, his stiff stature outlined against the dim hallway. "Mr Beaumont is here, Your Grace," he said, his voice low and respectful.

Alice's stomach fluttered. She wasn't expecting to see Ben Beaumont again tonight. Had he and George located Charlie already? But George had only just finished for the night, so...

"Show him in, please, Pratt."

Ben Beaumont stepped through the doorway, his bowler hat under his arm. A hint of urgency sharpened his usually calm blue eyes. "Good evening, Your Grace," he greeted, walking towards her. "I have some news that I think you will find interesting."

"Speak," Alice commanded, setting down her glass with a soft *clink*.

"It's rather contradictory to what we were led to believe." Ben rubbed his chin thoughtfully. "I met someone in the inn who was a passenger from the ship that Rydal and Fairfax sailed from India on. He says he saw the Earl of Foxworth and a young man together frequently throughout the journey. His description matched that of Charlie."

Alice nodded. It was all falling into place.

"But he also said they were with an older gentleman often too—a relative of the young man's, he thought. His description matched Lester Fairfax's."

Alice's brows furrowed. She had assumed Fairfax was unaware of his nephew's acquaintance with Foxworth. But now... "So if Fairfax *was* aware of their friendship, then why did he claim Charlie knew no one in London?"

"That's what I was wondering too, Your Grace."

"Perhaps it was an oversight. Although..." Alice then told Ben what she'd learned about Foxworth from Aunt Cora. "So surely, if Foxworth was attempting to convince Charlie to invest in his latest project, his uncle would've discouraged him from the association?" she pointed out.

"*If* he knew about it, Your Grace."

He has a point. Foxworth could have saved the 'business talk' until he was alone with Charlie.

Unless, of course, she was wrong, and this had nothing to do with his gold mines and all to do with keeping the young man from claiming his inheritance. And that led her back to Lady Rivershore and Henry Somerset.

"There's something else, Your Grace," he said. "A chambermaid at The Carlton told me she saw Mr Rydal leaving the hotel on late Saturday afternoon. Said he didn't look… well."

Alice's heart skipped. "What do you mean?"

"She claimed he was pale and unsteady and that a footman all but carried him into the carriage outside."

Alice frowned. "Drunk?"

"That's what the maid assumed. But a porter tells a different tale—he insists Mr Rydal looked frightened and that he heard him say he didn't want to go."

Alice's eyes narrowed. "The boys Holmes had watching the hotel—"

"They reported no struggle, Your Grace," Beaumont answered, "only saying that Rydal left the hotel, met the earl's carriage, and got in. He stumbled a little, and the footman offered an arm. No sign of force."

"So which version is true?"

Beaumont gave a half-shrug. "That, Your Grace, is the mystery."

Alice's heart rate quickened. "It could still be a kidnapping, do you think? Is the earl working with Lady Rivershore or Henry Somerset?"

"It's possible, Your Grace."

"Tomorrow first thing, Aunt Cora will request an audience with Lady Rivershore," Alice told him. "I'll attempt to find out if she or her son had a hand in this. In the meantime, George may find out the whereabouts of the Earl of Foxworth. I hope by tomorrow afternoon we will have a clearer picture of where Charlie Rydal is... And whether he's there by choice or force."

"Indeed. Goodnight, Your Grace." With a bow, Ben left.

Alice took a last sip of her port. *Tomorrow will bring answers*, she hoped. She just needed her aunt's request to see Lady Rivershore granted.

8

———

THE NEXT MORNING…

The subtle clink of china filled the air as Aunt Cora took a sip of her tea. "Alice, stop staring at the door," she scolded over breakfast in the morning room of Darby House. "It's far too early to expect a reply from Catherine." She returned her cup to its saucer, then scooped up a large spoonful of scrambled eggs from the silver dish in the middle of the table and dropped it onto her plate. Returning the spoon, she picked up the tongs and added two slices of crispy bacon to her eggs. "Just try to enjoy your breakfast," she said, returning the tongs to the dish.

Alice sighed. Aunt Cora was right. Lady Rivershore probably hadn't even woken up yet…

"Your warm scone, Your Grace." Pratt placed a plate in front of her, then added small dishes of jam, butter, and cream to the table.

"Thank you, Pratt," she said to the butler as he bowed, then left the room.

She remembered with a sliver of excitement that it was George's day off today. She buttered her scone absentmindedly. *Has he made any progress with Foxworth's household*

53

yet? The muffled sound of the clock striking nine in the hall reminded her it was probably too early for that as well. She added some jam and cream, then took a bite of her scone. She felt like they were so close to finding out what had happened to Charlie Rydal. And yet—

Pratt cleared his throat as he appeared in the doorway. His posture was rigid and his eyes filled with urgency. "Apologies for the interruption, ma'am." He bowed to Alice. "But a footman is at the courtyard entrance enquiring if you will receive the Countess of Rivershore."

What? Alice frowned as her eyes darted to meet Aunt Cora's, which were wide in surprise. "Er, yes. Pratt. Please tell him we will be delighted."

"Very well, ma'am," Pratt said, disappearing from sight as swiftly as he'd arrived.

"Well, that's unexpected. Why on earth is she sneaking around in our courtyard?" Alice asked Aunt Cora.

Her aunt seemed to have composed herself and considered the situation. "I think Catherine is likely being discreet because of her mourning. It wouldn't do for her to be seen visiting so soon after her husband's passing."

Of course! But then why the haste? Alice furrowed her brow, turning to Aunt Cora. "What did you say to persuade her to rush over here so early?"

"I simply told her we had news about her husband's nephew," she admitted, a hint of concern in her voice. "I do hope you know what you are going to say to her, Alice?"

Alice swallowed. She'd hoped to have had more time to prepare for this encounter. She could hardly accuse the dowager countess of kidnapping her husband's nephew with no further evidence other than that of their brief meeting at the hotel. And likewise, she would need to be careful that she didn't imply too strongly that Lady Rivershore's son had made Charlie disappear either.

"The Countess of Rivershore, Your Grace." Pratt had barely got his announcement out when Lady Rivershore swept into the room.

There was no more time for Alice to prepare.

The countess' usually composed face was now etched with worry. Without any preamble or pleasantries, she asked, "What do you know about my late husband's nephew?"

Alice dismissed Pratt as she moved over to greet the countess. The morning light flickering through the windows cast a shadow on the woman's distressed face. "Please take a seat, Your Ladyship." Alice gestured to the round dining table.

Looking for a second as if she would refuse, the countess let out a sigh, then moved to join Aunt Cora, who was already pouring her a cup of tea. Lady Rivershore took it as she settled herself, then she turned to Alice. "Well?"

"Charlie Rydal's staying at The Carlton, having sailed over from India with his uncle, Lester Fairfax." Alice deliberately said 'is' rather than 'was'. She wanted to know if Lady Rivershore knew he wasn't there at the moment.

Her ladyship attempted to feign surprise but did a poor job. She looked away and took a sip of her tea.

Deciding to be forthright, Alice continued as she walked towards the table. "But then, you already knew that, did you not? You went to the hotel using your maid's name and met with him."

Aunt Cora gave a sharp intake of breath as Lady Rivershore looked up at Alice, startled. Alice held the countess' gaze as she took the chair opposite her.

The countess took a deep breath, her fingers trembling as she cradled the porcelain teacup. "Robert's lawyers checked the ship's manifesto from twenty years ago, when his brother left for India," she said, her voice wavering. "Charlie Rydal was listed as a passenger, both leaving England and arriving in India."

"So he survived the voyage then?" Aunt Cora asked.

Lady Rivershore nodded. "It would appear so. They're still trying to find out what happened to him after that. But"—she shook her head—"the trail has gone cold."

Alice leaned forward, her eyes wide with curiosity. "So what prompted you to go to the hotel?"

"I couldn't resist seeking out Lester Fairfax when I heard he was in town and staying at The Carlton. I wanted to find out if he knew what had happened to the boy. But the clerk informed me he 'd gone out of town on business for a few days. Imagine my shock when he then told me that Lester Fairfax's nephew was also staying there if I wished to speak with him instead." She paused, taking a sip of tea to steady herself. "I thought I would swoon. My worst nightmare was coming true. Robert's rightful heir was here and waiting to claim his inheritance. And after everything Henry has worked so hard for—" Her voice hitched, and she took a second to regain her composure. "But curiosity won out in the end. I wanted to see him—the man who holds my and my son's fate in his hands." She clenched her jaw, then she let out a deep sigh. "But when I met him in the hotel library, well, he's no man. He's a boy." She slowly shook her head. "I didn't want to reveal my identity to him, so I told him I had a message for his uncle. He offered to take it, but I declined and left."

Alice could sense the desperation in the countess' voice. *It must have been so difficult to come face to face with her husband's heir like that.*

"I can imagine you must have been quite alarmed, Catherine," Aunt Cora said, reaching over and patting her friend's arm. "Did you tell Henry?"

Nicely done, Aunt...

"Indeed," Lady Rivershore admitted, her eyes betraying her fear. "I confided in him as soon as I got home."

And?

"He seemed entirely unruffled," she continued. "He assured me it wasn't over yet, and that he was working on a plan."

What does that mean? A plan to kidnap Charlie? Or even kill him? Alice's heart was beating in her ears. "Does Henry know the Earl of Foxworth?" Alice asked.

The countess put down her teacup and frowned. "Wasn't there some trouble with him a few years back?" She appeared genuine in her response.

"Yes, an investment scheme that went wrong and left several of the *ton* out of pocket," Aunt Cora explained.

"I remember Robert talking about it at the time. As for if Henry knew him, I think it's highly unlikely. Henry has spent this season in London, but prior to that he was learning to manage our estates, so was mostly in the country." She turned to Alice. "Why do you ask?"

Why indeed! Her mind was blank. Seconds seemed to stretch into minutes. She rested her fingers on the edge of her mouth and ran them along her lips. She was saved by Aunt Cora.

"So, Catherine, have you spoken to Lester, who presumably is now back?"

Alice shot her aunt a grateful look.

"No. Henry told me to be patient and not make any further contact with either of them." Lady Rivershore's hands trembled as she clasped them together, her voice now barely above a whisper. "I know Charlie's presence in London is bound to get out soon. Perhaps even before Friday. But please, I beg you both, don't speak of this conversation to anyone."

"Of course," Alice reassured her, feeling a swell of pity for the woman before her. Aunt Cora nodded her agreement, and with a final, nervous glance, Lady Rivershore rose, hastily took her leave, and left the room.

As soon as the door closed behind her, Alice turned to her aunt, her mind sifting through the remnants of their conversation. "Well, she was surprisingly open and honest," she said, returning to her seat. *Is it superb acting to disguise nefarious doings? Or does the countess genuinely think Charlie Rydal is alive and well and will claim his inheritance the day after tomorrow?*

"She seemed very distressed," Aunt Cora replied, concern etched on her face. She raised her chin. "It seems very unlikely to me that Catherine had anything to do with Charlie's disappearance."

Alice was inclined to agree. Her aunt had known Lady Rivershore for many years and was an excellent judge of character. If Aunt Cora thought her friend wasn't involved, then Alice believed her. Her eyes narrowed. "But what about her son, Henry?"

Aunt Cora considered this for a moment, then inclined her head. "It's possible, but would he truly be so ruthless?"

"Desperation can drive people to extreme measures," Alice replied, her mind racing through the possibilities. "If he feared losing what he thought was his by right and was facing the prospect that he and his mother were soon to be at the mercy of someone unknown to them, then…" She trailed off.

But if Henry Somerset didn't know Foxworth, then why had Charlie been seen going off in the man's carriage? She sighed. She needed to know where Charlie was…

9

LATER THAT AFTERNOON…

Alice sat alone in the conservatory at the rear of Darby House, her eyes idly tracing the sensational sketches on the front of Saturday's *The Illustrated Police News*. Away from the capital's distant bustle at the front of the house and surrounded by plants, the room, with its large windows, looked out on a serene walled garden. Within it, the gentle babbling of a fountain that fed the pool in the centre offered a relaxing backdrop.

Or at least it should have done.

Alice's mind was in turmoil. *Where's Charlie Rydal? Who's taken him?* Her stomach dropped. *Is he alive, even?*

There was a sharp knock on the door. "Come!" she called out.

Pratt entered. "Your Grace, George has requested an audience for him and Mr Beaumont."

George? On his day off? Her pulse quickened. She put down the paper. "Show them into the library, please, Pratt. I'll join them shortly." She rose, smoothing the fabric of her dress with palms that felt slightly clammy.

A few minutes later, the door to the library swung open with a brisk creak as Alice entered the room.

George, his posture ever-commanding, was standing by the window, while Ben Beaumont was scanning the bookshelves. He turned abruptly, and his eyes settled on Alice. "Your Grace," Ben said, tucking his bowler hat under his arm as he gave a quick bow. "We have news." He turned to George, who was now hovering beside him, and gave the off-duty footman a sharp nod.

Alice studied their faces. They didn't have the look of men about to announce bad news. *This bodes well...*

George stepped forward. "Your Grace." He bowed, then straightened. "The Earl of Foxworth's butler didn't appear last night at the club, but this morning when I returned, I was fortunate to find him there having breakfast. He told me the earl left for his country estate, Foxworth Hall in Richmond, on Saturday with a guest in tow."

Charlie Rydal! "That must be where Charlie is," Alice said, her eyes dancing.

"Indeed," Ben continued, his voice steady. "I contacted the household just a short while ago and can confirm he's quite the honoured guest there."

He's alive! A sigh of relief escaped Alice's lips as she pressed a hand to her chest. "That's wonderful news." She beamed at the two men. "Well done, both of you."

Then she paused. *A guest?* So her theory that Foxworth had him there to persuade him into buying into his gold mine scheme was likely true. *Let's just hope we're quick enough to stop Charlie before he signs away his fortune!* "We need to let his uncle know as soon as possible."

She moved to a desk in the middle of the room, where a delicate inkwell and a fountain pen were waiting. Taking a seat in the upholstered writing chair, she pulled out a sheet of her monogrammed stationery from the drawer and quickly penned a note to Lester Fairfax. After blotting the ink, she folded the note and sealed it with wax, using her family's crest. "Mr Beaumont, would you be kind enough to take this to Lester Fairfax at The Carlton?" She tilted her head to one side. "I have urged him to retrieve the boy posthaste."

Beaumont took the note, nodding firmly as he bowed. "At once, Your Grace."

"Thank you," she said to him, then turned to her footman. "Please enjoy the rest of your day off, George." He smiled, then bowed and followed the investigator out of the room.

Alice gave a slow smile. *Success!* Then her chest tightened. She rubbed her nose and sighed. *But now Charlie Rydal will claim his inheritance, and Lady Rivershore and Henry Somerset will be at his mercy.*

She walked over to the armchair by the window and slumped into it, all energy draining from her body. *I wish I never got involved in finding the earl's heir!*

***

The drawing room was bathed in a soft glow as Alice stood by the mantlepiece, a pained expression on her face as she tried to make sense of the events of the last few days. In retrospect, it seemed to her it had all been a big fuss about nothing. She rubbed her temple where a headache was threatening and wished she could skip dinner and retire to the quietness of her bedchamber to rest.

She sighed. Charlie Rydal hadn't been in any danger. He'd simply failed to inform his uncle he was going out of town as the guest of a mutual acquaintance. Without her involvement, although he may have signed away a part of his future fortune, he would have, no doubt, come back of his own accord in time to claim his place as the new Earl of Rivershore.

While this made her feel less guilty about her part in Lady Rivershore's unfortunate situation, she rather resented Lester Fairfax for having drawn her into this non-event. She'd been too ready to go along with the idea that Charlie had been abducted. She huffed. *The idea seems so ridiculous now.*

"Are you quite well Alice?" Aunt Cora eyed her from her chair by the window, where she'd been waiting patiently for dinner to be announced.

"I just feel—" Alice was interrupted by Pratt entering the room. *Ah, dinner...*

However, rather than announce that dinner was now served, he handed her an envelope. "This was just hand-delivered from The Carlton, Your Grace. I thought it might be important."

"Thank you, Pratt." Alice took it, breaking the seal.

"Well?" Aunt Cora rose and joined her.

Alice read out loud.

To Her Grace, The Duchess of Stortford
Darby House, Mayfair

Your Grace,

I am most pleased to inform you that Charlie is now safely returned to me at the Carlton. I am sincerely grateful for your kind attention in this matter and deeply regret any inconvenience my nephew may have caused through his thoughtless decision to accept an invitation to Foxworth Hall without leaving word of his intentions.

We shall wait upon Your Grace tomorrow morning to offer our apologies in person.

I have the honour to remain,
Your Grace's obedient servant,
The Right Honourable Lester Fairfax

"Well, I think that's the least they can do!" Aunt Cora barked as she plucked at her bodice. "It's a sorry affair for Catherine and young Henry now, that's for sure."

"Quite," Alice agreed, her thoughts drifting to Sherlock Holmes. *Has he got any closer to finding out if Lester Fairfax is involved in the stealing of The Nizam Blaze anklet and other artefacts?*

10

THE NEXT MORNING…

The early light cast a golden hue across the morning room's mahogany surfaces as Alice sat immersed in her correspondence to her husband. The scratch of her pen on paper mingled with the distant rumbling of carriages making their way through Mayfair, coming through the partly opened window. She paused, rereading the lines that called attention to his need to be discreet about his amorous goings-on—a matter she would much rather not have had to discuss with him.

She sighed. *This is partly your own fault, Alice.* After all, she'd been the one to leave Vance to his own devices in the country while she had quietly established a separate life for herself in London. She carried on writing.

I believe the time has come for us to speak plainly regarding our future. I trust we shall have opportunity for a private conversation when we are both at Francis Court next week. Though my father's birthday festivities will rightly occupy much of our attention, I am certain we might still afford one another sufficient time to arrive at an arrangement that serves us both—and does not render us the subject of idle speculation in London drawing rooms!

About to sign off the letter with a flourish, she hesitated. *What if I've entirely misjudged this?* She pressed a palm to her temple. Could her future with her husband become more than just them keeping out of each other's way until one of them died?

She stood and wandered over to the window. Was she truly prepared to make an effort to salvage her marriage? She paused, allowing the gentle breeze coming through the lace panels to wash over her. Deep down she knew what the correct answer was; she needed to—

"We don't have time for this, Fairfax. We're already behind schedule. My instructions were clear: no detours." A man's gruff voice drifted up from the street below.

Fairfax? Alice flattened herself against the wall and leaned slightly closer to the open window.

"It'll take fifteen minutes, no more, I assure you. But if all goes to plan, and I'm to integrate back into the *ton*, then this connection's important," Lester Fairfax replied, his voice strained but determined.

Connection? She wrinkled her nose. *Is he talking about me?*

"This is not about your social standing, Fairfax. We're delivering—not dawdling."

That's not Charlie Rydal, is it? The man certainly did not sound like someone of twenty-two.

"Exactly why we must not raise suspicion," Fairfax said sharply. "I have to call. Being seen by the Duchess of Stortford does wonders for one's respectability, don't you know."

Yes, I imagine I do, but I'm not sure I want to help you any more...

There was a pause. The other man muttered something Alice couldn't catch, followed by a disgruntled snort. "Fine. You have ten minutes. And keep your hand out of your coat pocket, for God's sake."

Who is this man? And why must Fairfax keep his hand out of his pocket?

"I know what I'm doing," Fairfax said, a touch of irritation in his voice. "Let me handle the duchess."

Handle me? She huffed. *I'm not a carriage horse in need of steadying.*

Their footsteps retreated, and a moment later, Alice heard the front bell ring.

Something odd is happening. She crossed the room with measured steps and resumed her seat, though her mind was anything but composed. Could this urgent errand Fairfax was running—this mysterious delivery—have something to do with the stolen artefacts Sherlock Holmes was chasing?

A subtle creak of the door opening announced the arrival of George. "The Right Honourable Lester Fairfax to see you, Your Grace," he declared, his deep voice resonating within the confines of the stately room.

She rose from the small writing desk by the window as Fairfax swept into the room, the morning light casting shadows across his drawn face.

Alice looked behind him, but no Charlie Rydal followed.

Her eyes narrowed slightly. Hadn't Fairfax's note last night said they would both be calling? She pressed her lips tightly together. She'd been keen to meet the young man who all this fuss had been about.

"Your Grace," Fairfax greeted with a stiff nod, his voice betraying a hint of unease.

"Mr Fairfax," she replied, moving gracefully around the mahogany desk. "I'd hoped to see your nephew with you today."

"Ah, yes, about that…" He faltered, the corners of his mouth twitching downward. He cleared his throat. "The boy rather overindulged during his stay at Foxworth Hall." His bushy moustache bristled. "He's still abed, I'm afraid."

"Indeed?" Alice arched an eyebrow. Her eyes held Fairfax's flustered gaze. *Or did young Charlie decide he couldn't face the consequences of his discourteous actions and refuse to come?*

"Regrettably, I couldn't delay my visit for him." Fairfax's hand drifted to his coat pocket. He patted it gently. A faint clinking noise whispered from within the fabric.

Alice's gaze moved to his coat, and he immediately snatched his hand away.

"Important business?" Alice asked, her curiosity piqued by the peculiar sound.

"Quite," he replied tersely, the creases around his eyes more visible as they darted towards the door.

There was no doubt Fairfax was more jumpy than a pheasant during the shooting season. *What are you up to?* "Please take a seat, Mr Fairfax." She gestured towards a plush couch near the hearth, her voice firm yet cordial.

Fairfax hesitated. Alice suppressed a smile, knowing the man outside would be eagerly waiting Fairfax's return but also knowing the heir's uncle did not want to offend her.

He agreed with a curt nod, then crossed the room, his movements careful, almost guarded. Another tinkle as delicate as a crystal chandelier swayed by a breeze reached Alice's ears.

She stood still. *What's that?*

Fairfax nervously rested his hand on the pocket of his morning coat as he sat down.

What is in his pocket? It sounded like small bells jangling together.

She froze as realisation dawned on her. *He doesn't, does he?* It would certainly explain the important business he could not delay…

Her heart raced. What should she do? She looked over at George standing by the side of the open door, but he seemed oblivious to her dilemma. There was a chance he hadn't heard it…

She bristled as she recalled Fairfax's comments outside just now. *Connection, indeed! Handle me, will he?* If she could help the great Sherlock Holmes expose Lester Fairfax as a thief and a smuggler, then she would do so! *I need a plan. So...* She needed to keep Fairfax here and get word to Sherlock Holmes. *Yes!* Her stomach flipped. But how would she do that without alerting Fairfax to what she was up to? *Tea. And George. Yes. That will work.* "I hope you'll stay and have tea, Mr Fairfax? I'm keen to hear how young Charlie is after his adventures in Richmond."

He stared sheepishly at her. "Once again, Your Grace, I can only apologise for the trouble his decision to go off without warning has caused." He shifted in his seat. "Er, about tea. I'm in a bit of a—"

She cut him off immediately. "Excellent. I'll arrange it now!" Before Fairfax had time to protest, she walked over to George, who was standing guard by the door.

She knew Fairfax and the man had to be somewhere soon. Well, not if she had anything to do with it! "Can we have tea for two, please, George?" She leaned in and whispered, "Ask someone to go with an urgent message to Sherlock Holmes at 221B Baker Street. Tell them to ask him to come immediately. Let him know I think I've found one of his missing artefacts."

He gave a curt nod. "Tea it is, ma'am."

Alice straightened up and smiled. "Thank you, George."

He turned gracefully and left the room.

She swivelled on her feet and ambled back to Fairfax, who was perched on the edge of the green sofa, his hands clasped in his lap as he stared at the door. Now she needed to keep him occupied while her message was delivered. She sat down opposite him and plastered a look of interest on her face. "So explain to me again why the Earl of Foxworth was so keen to spend time with your nephew, Mr Fairfax."

She zoned out as he repeated his story of their meeting with the earl on their voyage from India to England. She was in the process of stifling a yawn when Pratt and George entered with the tea things. Fairfax stopped talking as the men arranged the tea on the low table between her and him.

Much to her relief, they drank their tea in silence. Alice sipped hers slowly, conscious that time was running out for her to detain Fairfax much longer without raising his suspicions. He, on the other hand, gulped his down, his face trying but failing to disguise the discomfort of the hot tea as it burned its way down his throat.

She heard the front door open and the murmur of voices. Was that someone returning with a message? Or dare she hope it was Sherlock Holmes already? "More tea, Mr Fairfax?"

He placed his cup on the table, and he shook his head. "I've already taken up too much of your time, Your Grace."

He began to rise, but Alice waved him back down. *He can't leave yet.* "Nonsense, Mr Fairfax. I have some questions to ask you about life in India. I've always been fascinated by Asia."

The poor man slumped back in his chair, a resigned look on his face. Just then there was a sharp knock on the drawing room door. Pratt entered. "Pardon the interruption, Your Grace, but there's a rather persistent caller at the front door claiming to have a message from your brother. They adamantly refuse to speak with anyone but you."

Her heart skipped a beat. *Well done, Pratt.* She rose.

So did Fairfax. "I really should be leaving anyway, Your Grace. I—"

She waved him back down again. "Please, Mr Fairfax. My brother's quite accomplished at manufacturing disasters out of nothing at all. I'm confident it will not take long. Please help yourself to more tea. I'll be back momentarily."

She gave him no opportunity to protest as she hurried towards the door. Passing George, she gave him a look that she hoped conveyed her wish for him to keep an eye on Fairfax and not let him leave.

"Mr Holmes and a police gentleman are in the library, ma'am," Pratt said in a low voice as he escorted Alice down the corridor.

"Thank you, Pratt. I need you to do something for me, please." She gave him an instruction as she swung left at the lobby and entered the room at the end of the hallway. She was greeted with the scent of aged paper mingled with the faint aroma of polished wood as she closed the door behind her.

Over by the grand oak desk, in the centre of the room, stood a short man with a bushy moustache whom she didn't recognise. The tall figure of Sherlock Holmes emerged from the back of the room where rich mahogany bookcases lined the walls, filled to the brim with everything from classic literature to rare books. In his hand she recognised the leather-bound first edition of Isaac Newton's *Principia.* "You've an extensive collection of books here, Your Grace," he said, his eyes shining.

Alice smiled. "My maternal grandfather fancied himself a great scholar, Mr Holmes."

He dipped his head. "The Duke of Ross was known as a scientific forward thinker, I believe."

So he knows who my grandfather is? He'd obviously done his research on her. She stifled a huff. That meant he probably knew all about her faithless husband as well. She raised her chin.

Holmes strode over to the desk, placed the book carefully on the red leather top, and turned to the other man, who was now standing by his side. "May I introduce you to Inspector Gregson of Scotland Yard? Gregson, this is Her Grace, the Duchess of Stortford."

"Your Grace." The inspector bowed his head.

"Inspector. I assume you're working with Mr Holmes on the stolen Indian artefact case?"

He nodded.

"Well, I may be able to help you, gentlemen. Currently in my drawing room is The Right Honourable Lester Fairfax, who I believe has The Nizam Blaze in the left pocket of his morning coat."

"Well, I'll be dam—" Holmes coughed, interrupting the inspector.

Pratt appeared at the door and gave Alice a sharp nod.

"Of course, I cannot be absolutely sure, inspector," Alice continued, "but Pratt here will accompany you both to the drawing room where you may talk to Mr Fairfax and take what ever steps you feel are appropriate."

"Thank you, Your Grace," Holmes said, steering the inspector towards the door, where Pratt stood waiting.

"Oh, and one last thing, Mr Holmes. There's a man

outside the house. One of my footman is maintaining a close eye on him as we speak. I have reason to believe he's escorting Mr Fairfax somewhere with the stolen anklet."

Gregson's mouth dropped open. "I... I..."

"Come on, Inspector," Holmes said, steering the wide-eyed police inspector towards the door. "Let's see what these two men have to say for themselves, shall we?"

11

———

AN HOUR LATER…

E xtract from *The Society Page* broadsheet:

Rivershore Heir Recovered After Mysterious Absence

It has come to our attention that the long-anticipated heir to the Rivershore title arrived in London nearly a week past, accompanied by a discreet relation and reportedly lodging in a quiet Mayfair establishment. However, whispers soon spread that the young gentleman had vanished without explanation, prompting considerable consternation among those with an interest in the late earl's affairs.

Certain sources, not unfamiliar with the workings of the legal world, suggest that there were fears the heir had been deliberately removed from town in an effort to prevent his appearance at the official reading of the late Earl of Rivershore's will—scheduled to take place on the morrow.

Happily, the matter appears to have been resolved. The heir was located yesterday, alive and well, just beyond the city limits and was promptly returned to the Capital under quiet but careful supervision. It is now understood that he is under constant protection, presumably to deter any further attempts to obstruct his rightful claim to the title and entailed estates.

Meanwhile, speculation continues as to whether Mr Henry Somerset, the late earl's stepson, intends to pursue his previously hinted challenge to the entail. Whether such a move would gain traction—or sympathy—remains to be seen.

We shall report further as events unfold.

***

"Preposterous," Alice muttered under her breath as she threw down the copy of *The Society Page* on the sofa beside her in the drawing room at Darby House. Her green eyes narrowed, disbelief etched across her features. *Charlie Rydal was never in any real danger.* She plucked at the end of her sleeve. *The only protection he needs is from himself!* She clenched her hands, then slowly loosened them as she took a deep breath, letting it out through her nose.

The morning light cast shadows over the report next to her, which detailed the safe return of the missing heir, a story that felt wrong down to her very bones. *And,* she thought, *how could* The Society Post *possibly know so many details?*

She frowned. Who benefited from this story being made public? Her mind shifted through the possibilities. As she discarded one after another, there remained only one answer…

She grabbed the broadsheet and rose quickly. A sense of being used, a pawn in someone else's game, gnawed at her insides. She strolled across the room, then sticking her head around the door that was already ajar, she called out, "George!" the single word cutting through the quiet hum of the house.

Rapid footsteps approached, and George appeared at the top of the corridor. He hurried towards her, his blue eyes betraying a hint of concern. "Is everything all right, Your Grace?"

"No," Alice declared without preamble, thrusting the broadsheet towards him as he stopped in front of her. She turned and retreated into the room. "This article about the heir—it reeks of manipulation."

"Indeed?" George skimmed the paper in his hands as he followed her in. His brow furrowed. "They make it sound as if someone tried to harm the heir, but—"

"Exactly! It's been twisted around for a reason, and I think I know why." She told George the theory that had unfurled in her mind. "And the surest way to confirm it is to learn who furnished this account to *The Society Paper*."

"Should I get Mr Beau—"

"So can you send for Ben B—"

Alice's shoulders dropped as she smiled at her footman. "Great minds think alike, George. Yes, please find Mr Beaumont for me."

George bowed, still grinning, and left the room.

Alice paced the length of the room, her footsteps a soft whisper against the oriental rug. She was confident she knew *how*. And she knew *who*. But she wasn't convinced she had a full understanding of *why*. It had to have been done for more than just the publicity, but the answer escaped her at the moment.

Overcome with weariness, she halted by the window and pressed a cool palm against the glass. *What piece of this intricate puzzle am I missing?*

12

HALF AN HOUR LATER...

Alice sat in a chair by the window in the drawing room clutching a cup of tea. Her mind was still trying to make all the pieces of the puzzle fit.

"Your post, Your Grace."

Pratt's deep voice wrenched Alice's attention from the view of the street.

The butler walked over to where she was sitting, holding aloft a silver tray with a single envelope on it. Alice's stomach fluttered in anticipation. *Is it from Mr Holmes informing me of the arrest of Lester Fairfax?* She knew from George that both Lester Fairfax and the gentleman outside had been quietly taken away by Inspector Gregson and Mr Holmes earlier, yet no further word had reached her since. She was most eager to learn whether her suspicions regarding Fairfax had proved correct.

"Thank you, Pratt." She accepted the letter, her fingers brushing against the crisp paper. Then she spotted the family crest. Her heart sank. Normally, she enjoyed her mother's letters, but today, her mind was on more pressing matters.

"Anything interesting?" Aunt Cora asked from the sofa

across the room in front of the spread of small sandwiches and plump scones that made up their afternoon tea.

"Just Mama," Alice told her as she rose, letter in one hand and teacup in the other. She joined her aunt, taking the couch opposite her. She placed her cup down next to a pot of thick whipped cream.

"And what does she have to say?" Aunt Cora asked.

Alice suppressed a smile. Her aunt and mother were avid corresponders; the sisters wrote to each other at least two or three times a week. *There can hardly be anything in this letter that Aunt Cora doesn't already know!* About to point this out to her aunt, Alice paused. Perhaps, like her, Aunt Cora, who she'd brought up-to-date with the Charlie Rydal/Lester Fairfax case while they'd waited for tea, needed something to keep her mind occupied while waiting for Ben Beaumont to report back.

"Shall we take a look?" Alice broke the seal and unfolded the letter. She skimmed her mother's familiar script as it weaved through topics to do with the household at Francis Court, giving Aunt Cora a summary as she went, before she settled on news of an outbreak of scarlet fever among the tenant families.

"Mother is concerned for the welfare of the tenant children who are suffering from scarlet fever," she told her aunt.

Aunt Cora sighed. "Yes, she told me all about it in her last letter. It is such a worry, I know. Your mother was saying that the elementary school in Francis-next-the-Sea has already been temporarily closed down, and all the children affected have been quarantined at home."

Alice read on, her mother's concern for the children bleeding through the ink. "Mama has been having cold compresses and herbal teas made up at the house and distributed to the tenants and servants who have sick children."

Such a perilous thing, Alice dear, these childhood illnesses, as you well know, she read. Alice's thoughts drifted back to her son Freddie, who'd had a bout of chickenpox last year. She could still see the red spots and blisters scattered across his small torso and hear his cries as he fought the urge to scratch. Despite Nanny's excellent care, the scars on the back of his neck, although beginning to fade now, were a testament to his struggle.

"At least it is not smallpox," Aunt Cora said, taking a sip of her tea. "Hopefully, with plenty of rest and supportive care, the children will recover."

I hope so. Alice continued reading as her mother wrapped up with a reminder that both she *and* Vance were expected next week at the family gathering for her father's birthday. *Yes, mother. I know!*

As she folded the letter in two, a memory surfaced unbidden, carrying the echo of something Lady Rivershore had said on their first visit. *Smallpox!* Her stomach fluttered. *Could that be it?*

"What is it, Alice? Is something wrong?" her aunt asked in alarm.

That would be a powerful why. But how would she prove it?

Crash! A teacup was placed on the table in front of her with some force. "Alice!" Aunt Cora's voice was urgent.

Alice looked up into her aunt's concerned eyes. "I'm sorry, Aunt... but I have an idea."

Aunt Cora's face flooded with relief as she raised an eyebrow. "Well, let me hear it then."

Alice met her Aunt's gaze, then leaning forward slightly,

she said, "Do you remember when Freddie had chickenpox…"

***

"Your Grace," George's voice sliced through her absorption like a knife. "Mr Beaumont's here."

Alice put down *The Mystery of a Hansom Cab* by Fergus Hume, which she'd been attempting to read for the last ten minutes, but if truth be told, had barely taken in a word of. "Send him in, please, George." She rose and moved across the library, towards the door, her pulse quickening with anticipation. Would his news support the theory she'd disclosed to Aunt Cora over afternoon tea?

George stood aside as Ben Beaumont strode into the room. His sharp, observant eyes met hers without hesitation. "The hotel was the source for the article, Your Grace," he declared, removing his bowler hat and bowing.

I'm right so far! "Rydal or Fairfax?" Alice asked, a slow smile spreading over her face.

"I can't say for certain, but it came from one of them. That much is clear."

So much for Lester Fairfax telling her at their first meeting that he needed his nephew's disappearance to be kept quiet to avoid a scandal. *Another lie…* "Then we're close to the heart of it all," she said, a flicker of triumph in her eyes. "Mr Beaumont, I need you to find someone for me. It may not be easy, but it's crucial." She gave him the details, and with a wave of his hat, he rushed from the room. *I hope he can find her in time…*

Alice swiftly returned to her desk. She refilled her pen

with ink and composed a note. "George," she called. The footman hurried over. "Ride to Richmond, please, and deliver this to the Earl of Foxworth. Wait for his reply. Time is of the essence."

"Understood, ma'am." George bowed, his determination clear in his stance.

As the door closed behind him, Alice gently bit her lip. Her limbs were tingling. *With a fair wind and a little luck, I will be able to stop a great injustice.*

13

THE NEXT DAY…

It was Friday morning and Alice stood in front of the huge mahogany door to Lady Rivershore's morning room, waiting for the butler to announce her. The ticking from a grandfather clock diverted her attention, and she looked around the hallway to locate the ticking… *Bong!* She winced as the clock struck the hour.

A man coughed loudly. She whizzed around, unclenching her jaw. "Please come this way, Your Grace." She released a breath as her pulse rushed in her ears.

Pull yourself together, Alice. She took a deep breath in through her nose and followed the butler into the room. As she slowly breathed out, her gaze fell upon the Countess of Rivershore, who sat stiffly, her hands folded neatly in her lap. She rose and gave Alice a weary smile. "Your Grace, how unexpected."

"I do hope I'm not intruding at such an early hour," Alice said, moving towards her hostess. She knew she was doing exactly that. But she felt sure the information she had justified the breaking of any social etiquette rules around calling times.

Lady Rivershore's large blue eyes flickered towards her, the light catching them just so, causing them to sparkle despite the shadow of worry that loomed behind the irises. "Not at all, Your Grace," she replied, her words laced with the thin veneer of society's expected pleasantries. "I do hope Cora is well?"

Alice smiled. "My aunt is indeed well. Thank you, Your Ladyship."

"Please take a seat. Would you like tea?"

"No, thank you. I'll not intrude for long. I know today is a difficult day for you."

The countess' posture straightened.

Just say it, Alice! "But I have something… some information that may prove useful to you—" Her heart pounded in her ears. "Charlie Rydal is a—"

Whoosh! The door swung open, revealing Henry Somerset. His entrance disturbed the air, sending a ripple through the room. He halted when he saw her, then gave a curt bow. "Your Grace. We weren't expecting visitors today." His voice contained a low rumble of disapproval.

Alice bristled. *I'm here to help you!*

"Henry," his mother interrupted. "Her Grace has *kindly* come because she has something that may be of help to us." She gave him a look that warned him to behave.

"Indeed." Henry looked skeptical, then shrugged. "I intend to challenge the entail, anyway. I'm awaiting important information from India that could change everything."

Alice studied him for a moment, noting the agitation in his voice and the determination etched across his handsome features. *Try again...* "I believe Charlie Rydal is a fraud." Lady Rivershore gasped as Alice reached into her reticule and withdrew a folded piece of paper. She extended it towards a rather stunned looking Henry Somerset. "You may find this witness statement from the *real* Charlie Rydal's nursemaid useful."

Henry took it, his brow creasing his forehead. "Er... what?" he asked, his voice laced with confusion.

She suppressed a smile. "I suggest you challenge the man claiming to be your late stepfather's nephew, Mr Somerset, and ask him to prove he's indeed who he says he is." She pointed to the paper he was holding. "That will prove if he's telling the truth or not."

Henry stared at her open-mouthed. Suppressing a smirk, she turned away from him and dipped her head to Lady Rivershore, who also looked a bit like a goldfish. "I must be on my way, Your Ladyship."

Then, whirling back around to Henry, she added, "Good luck, Mr Somerset," the corners of her mouth lifting ever so slightly.

Outside, the morning air was crisp. The sound of rustling leaves and birdsong filtered through the atmosphere as Alice stepped down onto the street from Rivershore House. As her carriage appeared around the corner, she hesitated for a moment, her heart beating in tandem with the approaching horses' hooves. She'd done what she could. *It is in their hands now....*

14

LATER THAT DAY...

Alice perched on the edge of the plush velvet settee in the drawing room of Darby House, her attention attuned to the *clip-clop* of horses' hooves, the creaking of carriage wheels, and the faint cry of a flower girl outside. Familiar and comforting sounds. She glanced at the clock on the mantel. *What's happening at the Rivershore's lawyers? Is the information I provided Henry Somerset enough to have Charlie Rydal declared an imposter?*

"Alice!"

Her eyes sprang open wide, the firm voice of her aunt pulling her out of her stupor.

"I asked if you wanted another crumpet?" Aunt Cora raised an eyebrow at her niece.

Alice took a deep breath in through her nose. *Focus!* She looked at the spread of afternoon tea delights that were laid out on the table and shook her head. "No, thank you. I've eaten more than enough."

"Can you believe your father will be sixty years old?" Aunt Cora mused, sipping her tea. "Francis Court will certainly be abuzz with activity next week when we're there

85

to celebrate his birthday. It will be good to be back in Fenshire for a few weeks. We'll all need a break once this ta-doo with Catherine is resolved…" She trailed off as she placed her cup on a side table.

Alice swallowed. She hoped she hadn't let Aunt Cora's friend down by her involvement in this Case of the Not-So-Missing Heir, as she was now referring to it. She looked down at her delicate ivory kid leather boudoir shoes and studied the row of tiny mother-of-pearl buttons that secured them snugly along the side. *Is Henry Somerset now the new earl?* She glanced up at Aunt Cora, who was jittering a foot against the floor. It seemed her aunt was as nervous as she was to find out the final outcome of the meeting between the man claiming to be Charlie Rydal and the earl's lawyers.

She smarted. *And to think I was worried that Charlie would sign away all his inheritance to that trickster, the Earl of Foxworth!* In fact, it was the earl who'd been used, not the other way around.

She could just imagine how delighted Fairfax and Rydal must have been to have met the earl on the ship and found out he'd been trying to gain investors for his new project. What a splendid way to set up their missing heir ruse—befriend a member of the aristocracy, tell him you were the heir to the Earl of Rivershore, and invite yourself to stay with him while your uncle made it subtly known among London society that you were missing. Lester Fairfax must've considered it a real bonus when he'd been referred to a duchess who could help him. The more people who believed that Charlie the heir was missing, the more they would believe Charlie *was* the heir.

And it had worked to start with. She herself had accepted Fairfax's story at face-value. As had Lady Rivershore when she'd gone to the hotel and met her husband's so-called nephew. Alice took a sip of her tea. And then, of course, there was the report in *The Society Page* that the heir had been found and the implication that he was in danger because he was the heir. All to legitimise his position. Alice stifled a huff. She'd been used!

Then Alice frowned. If Charlie was an imposter, was Lester Fairfax one too? Her stomach clenched. Sherlock Holmes had been sure Fairfax was trading in stolen artefacts, and she herself believed he had the stolen anklet in his possession when he had come to her house yesterday, so was it such a leap to imagine that given the opportunity, he was also involved in a deception to take the inheritance belonging to the *real* nephew of the late Earl of Rivershore?

A corner of her mouth twitched. Well, at least Fairfax—or whoever he was—would likely get his comeuppance if he *was* smuggling stolen goods.

And Charlie? She could only hope that his claim had been thrown out. Her limbs were still heavy as she lifted her teacup to her mouth again. *If I only knew what the ruling was…*

The crisp sound of Pratt's heels tapped against the wooden floor, making his presence known before his voice did. "Mr Henry Somerset to see you, Your Grace," he announced as he stopped just inside the doorway.

Teacup paused in mid-air, she turned to the doorway, a fluttering in her stomach. "Show him in, please, Pratt."

Alice set her teacup down with a soft *clink*, then rose. Smoothing down her bodice, she licked her dry lips. *Am I about to find out?*

Henry Somerset's entrance was as dashing as the man himself, his black hair slightly tousled from the brisk London air. With a crisp nod to Pratt, he stepped into the drawing room with the confidence of a man who knew his worth.

"Mr Somerset, what an unexpected pleasure," Alice greeted, attempting to keep the anticipation out of her voice.

Henry removed his hat as his gaze found Alice, holding her eye for a breath longer than necessary, before he bowed deeply. "Your Grace, I'm here to convey my deepest gratitude for your invaluable assistance."

A blush threatened her cheeks, but she maintained her composure.

Henry's lips quirked up in a half-smile, his brown eyes glinting with trust. "I also wanted to tell you about what happened earlier, after you were kind enough to provide us with such critical information," he said. "I trust you and your aunt will keep our conversation confidential." Alice and Aunt Cora both nodded. He bowed in return, then gave a wry smile. "Although, no doubt, my news will soon be common knowledge."

Alice tilted her head in agreement. Nothing stayed private within London society for long. She gestured for Henry to join them.

As they all settled into their seats, Henry accepted a steaming cup of tea from Aunt Cora with a nod of thanks, then he sat too.

"Charlie Rydal came alone to the meeting," he said, stirring his tea casually, though the tension in the room wound tighter with each word. "I expected his uncle would be with him," he told them, a frown furrowing his brow. "I cannot fathom why he was absent."

Alice and Aunt Cora shared a knowing look. *He was most likely still with the police.*

Henry continued, "Charlie seemed confident despite his uncle's absence. He proudly announced that he was Charles Rydal, and he was here to claim his rightful inheritance as laid out by the entail." He paused, no doubt for effect, then carried on, "However, when the lawyers challenged him with the information you'd provided, his demeanour faltered."

He raised an eyebrow at Alice. "What made you suspect he was an imposter?"

"The entire tale in *The Society Page* struck me as contrived. The implication that Charlie Rydal was somehow in danger felt staged," she answered.

"Staged?" Henry echoed, his brow furrowing again.

"Indeed," Alice continued. "I believe the article sought to merely confirm that Charlie was the rightful heir. I deduced that the only people who would benefit from such affirmation were Charlie and his uncle."

"A valid point," Henry conceded, leaning back in his chair.

"Subsequently, I considered the whole missing heir situation and wondered if it could've been a ruse to add legitimacy to their claim. I sent a message to the Earl of Foxworth, and he confirmed that Charlie Rydal had invited *himself* to visit the earl's home in Richmond, not the other way around."

It had all seemed so plausible at the time—Charlie leaving the hotel without a word, the whispers of his unwillingness to leave via that conflicting account about the footman. Charlie had "looked dazed or unsteady" one member of staff had said, while another had been certain the young man had resisted. Yet, Holmes's watchers had seen no such thing. Just a young man being helped into a coach.

She could imagine Charlie deliberately looking fearful, hoping that would get reported back when questions were asked later. Had he also pretended to stumble so that someone would help him into the carriage? To a witness who already believed that he was going reluctantly, it would appear to support the theory that he was being taken against his will. The illusion of danger had been subtly but expertly crafted.

Aunt Cora leaned forward. "I must confess, there was a time when we thought perhaps you and your mother had...

well, taken steps to ensure Charlie's claim didn't succeed, did we not, Alice?"

Aunt Cora!

Henry blinked, clearly startled. "You thought we'd kidnapped him?" His eyes meet hers.

She swallowed. *Actually, at one point, we thought you'd killed him!* Alice's cheeks grew hot as she gave him a sheepish shrug. "I saw you both in conversation on Tuesday just as we were leaving after our visit to Rivershore House. You told your mother, 'he's not going anywhere until I say so'." Alice's fingers twitched against her skirts. "It seemed suspicious."

He studied her for a beat, then his face cleared. "You saw us speaking after my mother's visit to the Carlton then. That explains it." He gave a short, humourless laugh. "I wasn't happy with her for going. I told her Charlie wasn't to be contacted again—not until we were certain who he was or what he wanted. She was terrified someone might find out she'd gone there in disguise, using one of the maids' names."

He leaned forward slightly, his voice soft. "That comment was about us controlling the narrative. I meant that we wouldn't let this claim move forward without evidence. And that we would deny everything about her visit if it ever came to light."

Alice exhaled slowly. "Of course, that makes sense in retrospect."

Henry tilted his head, a flicker of amusement in his eyes. "It's rather unsettling how much you can glean from a conversation no one meant you to hear."

Alice's neck was on fire as she took a sip of tea. *If he never speaks to me again, I'll not be surprised.*

"Well, we didn't believe it for long, did we, Alice? So no harm done," Aunt Cora said cheerily. "More tea?"

Henry shook his head. "No, thank you." He turned back to Alice, his face open and friendly. "So, returning to the broadsheet report, that's when you suspected he wasn't the rightful heir?"

Alice suppressed a sigh of relief. *He seems to have forgiven me for thinking him capable of kidnapping.* "Exactly," Alice agreed, tilting her head towards him. "His behaviour alone wasn't enough to prove he was a fraud. But I had a strong conviction that he was. It was a comment from my mother in her letter to me yesterday that proved to be the key. She was talking about an outbreak of scarlet fever among the tenants' children. That, in turn, reminded me of my own son's bout of chickenpox last year and the scars he'd been left with. I recalled your mother had mentioned young Charlie Rydal had had smallpox before they'd left for India."

"Ah, so you thought there might be lasting scars?" Henry smiled, dipping his chin in understanding.

"On the off chance that such scars might still be visible, my man tracked down the nursemaid who'd cared for Charlie prior to their departure for India. She confirmed he'd had terrible scarring on his back and remnants of them would likely remain even today."

"Your instincts were correct, Your Grace." Henry's dark eyes were serious, yet triumphant. "Charlie refused to be examined, but before the lawyers could insist, a telegraph arrived." He paused again, glancing between her and her aunt before continuing, "it was in response to a request for records from the British Consulate that I'd demanded the lawyers make."

"Go on," Aunt Cora urged, her hazel eyes wide with anticipation.

"According to the consulate," Henry said, barely able to

contain his satisfaction, "a child named Archibald Rydal died two weeks after arriving in India."

Alice frowned. "Archibald?"

"Yes, your grace. After checking the birth certificate, it turns out the real Charlie Rydal was actually born Archibald Charles. He was named after his paternal grandfather. However, his mother didn't care for the name, so he was called Charlie from the day he was born," Henry explained, his handsome features trying to contain a smile. "According to one of the lawyers who'd known the earl's younger brother very well, no one knew the child as anything other than Charlie."

But surely, Lester Fairfax would have known the real name of his nephew? That strengthened her belief that Fairfax was an imposter too.

"So the man purporting to be Charlie and the *real* Charlie's uncle, Fairfax, had assumed his name was Charles?" Aunt Cora asked, frowning.

"Indeed, Lady Dunmore. According to my mother, there'd been a falling out between Fairfax and his sister before Archibald had been born, and they'd only resumed contact six months before they'd left to go to India."

Oh. Alice's shoulders slumped. So the man calling himself Fairfax *could* still be the real uncle.

Henry continued, "In any case, the lawyer asked him to confirm his full name in writing, and then they presented him with a copy of the birth certificate. Upon realising his charade lay exposed, the imposter fled."

"Have they apprehended him?" Aunt Cora asked, shifting in her seat.

"Fortuitously, the police were waiting outside the offices" —Henry glanced at Alice and raised an eyebrow. She gave a sly smile in return— "and chased after him. I've no doubt they'll detain him soon."

Dispatching that note to Gregson had been a gamble; had she been mistaken, it might well have shattered her credibility with the inspector. Fortunately, her instincts had proved sound.

"So the entail is now broken?" Aunt Cora asked.

Henry nodded, smiling, and rose from his seat. "You see before you the new Earl of Rivershore." He gave a deep bow, then his gaze rested on Alice's face. "Your Grace, I must thank you most sincerely." There was a touch of admiration in his eyes. "Please allow my mother and me to express our gratitude properly by doing us the honour of dining with us tomorrow evening at Rivershore House."

Alice stood and offered him her gloved arm. "We shall be delighted to attend," she replied, a generous smile gracing her lips as he lingered just a moment too long over her fingers.

"Excellent," Henry said as he straightened. "I'll look forward to it."

Her stomach fluttered as she accompanied him to the door. Outside, Pratt was waiting. As the butler nodded and gestured for Henry to follow him, the new earl turned and added over his shoulder, "For what it's worth, Your Grace, kidnapping Charlie Rydal *was* briefly on the list." He winked, then disappeared down the corridor after Pratt.

Good gracious! Alice fanned her face as she watched him disappear from view. Suddenly, tomorrow evening held rather more promise than she had anticipated.

As she turned and re-entered the drawing room, her thoughts were already racing ahead to what she might wear for the occasion. She and her aunt would be the first to dine with the new Earl of Rivershore—a detail unlikely to escape the notice of London society.

15

THAT EVENING…

Alice sipped a glass of port in the library, glad of the peace and quiet now that Aunt Cora had withdrawn for the evening. She gave a deep sigh of satisfaction. She would send for Ben Beaumont in the morning and pay him for his help with the Case of the Not-So-Missing Heir. She'd already agreed with Pratt that George was to be given the day off on Sunday. The case was closed.

Although, I would love to know if the police have apprehended the man calling himself Charlie Rydal yet.

And what would become of the man claiming to be his uncle? *Is he really Lester Fairfax?*

She would write to Mr Holmes tomorrow and ask him to apprise her of the situation…

Alice's thoughts drifted back to the conversation she'd had with Aunt Cora earlier, after Henry had left.

"Will Vance be attending the celebrations for your father next week, Alice?" Aunt Cora had inquired as she'd sipped her sherry, her hazel eyes searching Alice's face for any signs of discomfort.

"Of course. Mother insists."

"I know I said he's a nincompoop. And I stand by that. But, at the end of the day, he *is* your husband." Aunt Cora had held Alice's gaze. "Perhaps it will be the perfect time to mend fences," she said, her tone gentle yet firm. "Your marriage might not be irreparable, my dear."

Recalling her aunt's words, Alice's stomach hardened. Hadn't her and Vance's distinct paths in life grown irreconcilably apart since the boys had left for school? Was there any point in trying to bridge the chasm after living separate lives for so long? And then there was his dalliance with her cousin…

The handsome face of Henry Somerset popped into her mind. His sparkling brown eyes as he'd hovered over her hand for just a little too long… If Vance could have his fun, perhaps she could too?

Alice! she scolded herself as she dragged her thoughts back to her marriage.

Is Aunt Cora right? Was there still hope for a reconciliation—a chance to rebuild their fractured union brick by brick?

But do I want to?

She took another sip of port, the liquid heating her throat as she swallowed. The worry about Vance would wait—after all, she had more immediate concerns, like what shoes would perfectly complement her gown for dinner at Rivershore House tomorrow night. *I think I'll wear my new pink satin slippers, the ones with the red roses on the top.*

16

THE NEXT MORNING...

"Mr Sherlock Holmes and Inspector Gregson, Your Grace," Pratt announced, standing to one side. The thin detective with the hawk-like nose strode into the morning room, looking formal in his tailored green wool suit, followed by the inspector, who was sporting an impressively full moustache and wearing a fitted morning coat in dark blue.

"Forgive us for arriving without an appointment, Your Grace," Holmes said as he stopped before Alice, "but we were eager to report the outcome of our recent inquiries."

A tingle travelled down her spine. Had they managed to prove that Lester Fairfax—or whatever his name was—was not all he claimed? And had they caught the man pretending to be Charlie Rydal? She turned to Pratt. "Tea, if you please, Pratt."

The butler bowed and left the room.

"Do sit, please, gentlemen." She indicated the sitting area by the fireplace. "I'm most interested to hear what has become of Lester Fairfax."

Gregson took a seat. "Mr Fairfax is presently being held

on charges of smuggling, violation of customs laws, and possession of stolen property. You were quite correct, Your Grace. He had The Nizam's Blaze in his pocket, just as you supposed." He raised an eyebrow at her as if inviting an explanation as to how she had known.

She ignored the silent enquiry, and instead asked, "And are you certain he's indeed Lester Fairfax, inspector?"

Gregson inclined his head. "We've verified his identity, Your Grace."

Oh. Alice suppressed a deep sigh. She'd been mistaken. *The real uncle's a conman as well as a thief...*

Gregson cleared his throat and continued, "He was not particularly forthcoming at first. He claimed it had all been a misunderstanding—that he was merely assisting a friend by delivering the anklet in person, after they'd acquired it directly from a seller in India." Gregson indicted Holmes, who was sitting in the armchair next to the settee, his legs crossed and his hands in his lap. "Fortunately, owing to the evidence supplied by Mr Holmes and his associates following their visit to Southampton, we were able to demonstrate that we possessed proof of his having used his tea export business as a means of smuggling stolen goods out of India. The evidence was irrefutable, and he ultimately confessed. He explained that, following the death of his brother-in-law— with whom he had shared equal partnership in the firm—he'd been obliged to seek alternative sources of income in order to purchase his sister's inherited share of the business."

"She had no shortage of opinions on how matters ought to be conducted," Holmes added, raising an eyebrow as a wry smile crossed his face.

Alice suppressed a grin. A woman with an opinion would likely terrify most men!

"He then protested ignorance of the goods' origins," Gregson scoffed. "He claimed he was merely providing a means of conveyance for certain associates in India as he already had tea consignments bound for England."

Alice frowned. Could Fairfax have been unwittingly embroiled in a much bigger operation? "Is that likely? Surely —" She paused when she heard the rattle of the tea tray, accompanied by the soft thud of footsteps on the carpet in the corridor outside. "Ah, here's tea."

Gregson and Holmes looked towards the door expectantly. A minute later, it opened to reveal Pratt with the tea things.

After the butler had laid out the items and left, Alice poured for both men. She attempted to make her observation again. "It seems unlikely to me that Fairfax would be unaware of the origin of his cargo. He didn't strike me as a stupid or gullible man." In fact, if, as she suspected, he'd been the orchestrator of the attempt to pass off someone as his nephew to get his hands on the late earl's wealth, then he was both clever and devious.

"He's neither, Your Grace." Holmes tapped his chin with his forefinger. "He informed us—rather smugly, in my estimation—that his nephew was soon to be the new Earl of Rivershore. At that point, Inspector Gregson and I agreed it would be best to leave him for a day to stew a while before speaking with him again last night."

Gregson gave a short laugh. "You may imagine, then, how fortunate it was that I received your note yesterday morning regarding your suspicions about the man calling himself Charlie Rydal, who was asserting a claim to the Rivershore estate. We kept him under observation after he left the earl's solicitor's office and apprehended him at Euston Station, just as he was attempting to quit the Capital for

Liverpool, where he had evidently hoped to secure passage back to India."

Alice's heart skipped a beat. *So they've caught the imposter!* Her head was filling up with questions. She suppressed the urge to blurt them out and instead allowed Gregson to continue.

"Upon being informed that his so-called nephew had failed in his attempt at fraud and was now in our custody, Mr Fairfax's demeanour altered considerably. He expressed a willingness to co-operate fully and entered a plea of guilty to charges of smuggling and customs evasion. Furthermore, he offered to disclose the details of the entire operation behind the stolen artefacts in India. In exchange, he requested that any charges pertaining to the conspiracy to defraud the Rivershore estate be withdrawn."

"Which was very helpful, as the other man we have detained was proving to be very tight-lipped," Holmes added.

So Fairfax had wanted to strike a bargain, had he? Well, that made sense. Once he'd realised the ruse had failed, he would have known that there were no rich relatives to smooth his path with the law. Perhaps all he could hope for now was that by pleading guilty, he could avoid a very public trial. After all, the newspapers would lap up the story of an earl's brother gone bad. It was smart of him to avoid all of that if he could. "And did you come to mutually agreeable terms, inspector?"

"Yes, Your Grace. We have long sought to uncover those responsible for the thefts. Dismantling their operation is a considerable success for Scotland Yard."

And it will no doubt reflect well on you too, inspector... She glanced over at Holmes, and he smirked.

So what about Charlie Rydal—or whoever he was? "So

was the man presenting himself as Charlie Rydal also involved in the smuggling and stolen goods enterprise?"

"Cedric Worth is his true name," Gregson told her. "His father's the senior manager at Fairfax's tea plantation. The boy was well-educated and rather ambitious, but he had no desire to follow in his father's footsteps. He aspired to live as a gentleman, without the inconvenience of earning his keep. So when Fairfax required someone to impersonate his deceased nephew, Worth was the right age—and more than willing to accept the payment."

He paused to take a sip of tea before continuing, "Fairfax maintains that neither his sister nor Worth was aware of the smuggling."

"Is that possible, inspector?"

"Worth's a young man of limited judgement and little inclination for honest work. I am convinced, upon speaking with him, that he had no knowledge of the broader scheme. He merely did as he was instructed by Fairfax."

"And what will happen to him now?" Alice asked.

"There will be no formal proceedings brought against him, but he shall be placed on the next ship bound for India. It has been made quite clear to him that he will not be welcomed back—now or ever." Gregson's bushy moustache bristled. "As for the Right Honourable Lester Fairfax, he'll be detained at Her Majesty's pleasure, either at Pentonville or Brixton. He's fortunate—his social standing spares him the less agreeable institutions."

Alice frowned. *Is that fair?* His social status would buy him a better life in prison than the next man? But then, she supposed, he hadn't killed anyone. So did he deserve to be with murderers and blackguards? Her temples began to throb.

Gregson took out his pocket watch, then rose. "If you'll

forgive me, Your Grace. I have some pressing business back at Scotland Yard." He glanced over at the door.

She and Holmes stood too. "Of course, inspector. I appreciate you both coming to inform me of the outcome."

The two men headed towards the door. As they reached it, Holmes stopped and swivelled around to face her. "It's been a pleasure to meet you, Your Grace." He gave her a quick bow. "I hope our paths cross again in the future."

17

———

EXTRACT FROM THE SOCIETY PAGE BROADSHEET. MONDAY 25 MAY 1891

<u>A Notable Supper at Rivershore House</u>

*I*t *appears that the ladies of the* ton, *eager to be among the first to dine with Lord Rivershore in his new capacity, have been quietly outpaced.*

On Saturday last, the newly elevated Earl was host to Her Grace, the Duchess of Stortford, at his residence in Belgravia. Also in attendance were the Duchess' aunt, the Countess of Dunmore, and the Earl's mother, the Countess of Rivershore.

That such an intimate gathering should occur so soon after the earl's succession has, unsurprisingly, given rise to murmurs among society. Some are beginning to wonder whether Her Grace, rather than hastening to confront her husband concerning his alleged entanglement with Lady Forthington, has elected instead to meet subtlety with subtlety —and to match the rumour with a quiet but notable appearance of her own.

18

EXTRACT FROM THE SOCIETY PAGE BROADSHEET. THURSDAY 28 MAY 1891

Society Turns East for the Duke of Arnwall's Birthday Celebrations

A considerable portion of London's fashionable set is preparing to depart for the east coast this week, where the 12th Duke of Arnwall is to celebrate his sixtieth birthday at his ancestral seat, Francis Court, in Fenshire.

Among the expected guests are his daughter, Her Grace, the Duchess of Stortford, and her husband, who have not, it is whispered, been seen together in society for over five months. Their anticipated reunion has given rise to no small amount of speculation.

Two questions appear to be occupying the minds of the ton: Will the Duke's niece—Lady Forthington, whose name has of late been linked rather too freely with that of the Duke of Stortford—be present at the gathering? And has an invitation also been extended to the newly titled Earl of Rivershore, who is said to harbour a particular admiration for the Duchess herself?

———

I hope you enjoyed *An Heir is Misplaced*. If you did, then please consider letting others know by writing a review on Amazon, Goodreads or both. Thank you.

Want to know how Alice's father's birthday celebrations at Francis Court go? The clue is in the title of the next book in this series… *A Husband is Hushed Up*, is available for pre-order now in your Amazon store.

Want to read more by me? Lady Beatrice is Alice's great-great-great niece on her father's side and is 17th in line to the (fictional) British throne. She is also a trouble magnet when it comes to murder! Find out how Bea and her sister's assistant (and future best friend) solved their first crime together. *A Toast To Trouble* is the introductory novel in the *A Right Royal Cozy Investigation* series and you can download the ebook for FREE when you join my readers' club at https://www.subscribepage.com/helengoldenauthor_bmatttrm or if you'd prefer you can buy the ebook or paperback in the Amazon store.

For other books by me, take a look at the back pages.

If you want to find out more about what I'm up to you can find me on Facebook at *helengoldenauthor* or on Instagram at *helengolden_author*.

. . .

Be the first to know when my next book is available.
Follow Helen Golden on Amazon, BookBub, and Goodreads
to get alerts whenever I have a new release, preorder, or a
discount on any of my books.

CHARACTERS IN ORDER OF APPEARANCE

AN HEIR IS MISPLACED

Alice, Duchess of Stortford — lives at Darby House, London. Wife of Vance. Mother of Harry and Freddie. Daughter of the Duke of Arnwall.

Vance, Duke of Stortford — lives at Manning Hall in Derbyshire. Husband of Alice. Father of Harry and Freddie.

Lilian 'Lilly', Lady Forthington — lives in Derbyshire. Widow of Sir Francis Forthington. Cousin of Alice. Rumoured paramour of Vance.

Sir Francis Forthington — late husband of Lilly.

Percival, Duke of Arnwall — lives at Francis Court, Fenshire. Alice's father.

Cora, Countess of Dunmore — lives at Darby House. Alice's aunt on her mother's side. Widow.

Harold 'Harry', Lord Threeble — older son of Alice and Vance. Away at school in Derbyshire.

Lord Frederick 'Freddie' Manning — younger son of Alice and Vance. Also away at school in Derbyshire.

Robert, Earl of Rivershore — late husband of Catherine and stepfather of Henry Somerset.

Catherine, Countess of Rivershore — recently widowed wife of Robert. Lives at Rivershore House in London. Mother of Henry Somerset via previous marriage.

Henry Somerset — Son of Catherine and her late first husband. Stepson of Robert. Inherits his stepfather's title and estate if no heir turns up by the deadline.

Lord James Astley — Alice's younger brother and youngest son of the Duke of Arnwall.

Pratt — Alice's butler at Darby House

Fiona 'Fee', Countess of Tilling — Married to Alice's older brother, Duncan. Alice's best friend.

The Right Honourable Lester Fairfax — Uncle of missing heir, Charlie Rydal.

George Stokes — Alice's lead footman

Charlie Rydal — Nephew of Robert, Earl of Rivershore and heir to his title and estates if he claims them before the deadline.

Ben Beaumont — Private investigator based in London.

Maud Willis — Alice's maid

Judith Willis — Maud's cousin who works for the Countess of Rivershore

Sherlock Holmes — Consulting detective residing at 221B Baker Street in London

Edward, Earl of Foxworth — Passenger on the same ship from India as Charlie Rydal and TRH Lester Fairfax.

The Duke of Ross — Alice's maternal grandfather.

Inspector Gregson — of Scotland Yard.

A BIG THANK YOU TO...

To my editor Marina Grout. Thank you for your insight, patience, and the perfect balance of encouragement and honesty.

To Ann, Ray, Lissie, and Carolyn for being my beta readers and/or additional set of eyes before I push the final button. I really appreciate your help in making my books the best version of themselves.

To my ARC Team. You are all brilliant! I really appreciate your feedback and your constant support.

To my fellow authors in the Cozy Mystery Writers' Clubhouse Group. Thank you for being a haven of advice, cheerleading, and therapy.

To you, my readers. Thank you for your loyalty, your enthusiasm, and your wonderfully suspicious minds.

As always, I may have taken a little dramatic license when it comes to Victorian police procedures, so any mistakes or misinterpretations, unintentional or otherwise, are my own.

BOOKS BY HELEN GOLDEN IN THIS SERIES

An introductory novella in the new
The Duchess of Stortford Mystries
series set in the 1890s and
featuring Alice, The Duchess of
Stortford.
When an heir to an earldom goes
missing Alice is asked to
investigate, but with the clock
ticking and the gossip swirling, can
Alice find the missing heir before
it's too late?

It's Alice's father's 60th birthday
and all of London high society has
descended on Francis Court for the
celebrations. But when Alice's
husband is found in a heap at the
bottom of the stairs, and the police
declare it an accident, Alice
believes it's murder. Helped by her
maid and footman, can she find out
what happened before the guests
disburse and a killer goes free.

PAPERBACKS AVAILABLE
FROM WHEREVER YOU BUY
YOUR BOOKS.

OTHER BOOKS BY HELEN GOLDEN

A novella lenght prequal in the series A Right Royal Cozy investiation series. With Perry and Bea working against each other, can they still save the party—or will it be ruined beyond repair along with Francis Court's reputation as a gold-standard venue?

A short prequal in the series A Right Royal Cozy Investigation. Can Perry Juke and Simon Lattimore work together to solve the mystery of the missing clock before the thief disappears? FREE novelette when you sign up to my readers' club. See end of final chapter for details. Ebook only.

First book in the A Right Royal Cozy Investigation series. Amateur sleuth, Lady Beatrice, must pit her wits against Detective Chief Inspector Richard Fitzwilliam to prove her sister innocent of murder. With the help of her clever dog, her flamboyant co-interior designer and his ex-police partner, can she find the killer before him, or will she make a fool of herself?

Second book in the A Right Royal Cozy Investigation series. Amateur sleuth, Lady Beatrice, must once again go up against DCI Fitzwilliam to find a killer. With the help of Daisy, her clever companion, and her two best friends, Perry and Simon, can she catch the culprit before her childhood friend's wedding is ruined? Also in Audio format.

The third book in the A Right Royal Cozy Investigation series. When DCI Richard Fitzwilliam gets it into his head that Lady Beatrice's new beau Seb is guilty of murder, can the amateur sleuth, along with the help of Daisy, her clever westie, and her best friends Perry and Simon, find the real killer before Fitzwilliam goes ahead and arrests Seb? Also in Audio format.

OTHER BOOKS BY HELEN GOLDEN

A Prequel in the A Right Royal Cozy Investigation series.
When Lady Beatrice's husband James Wiltshire dies in a car crash along with the wife of a member of staff, there are questions to be answered. Why haven't the occupants of two cars seen in the accident area come forward? And what is the secret James had been keeping from her?

When the dead body of the event's planner is found at the staff ball that Lady Beatrice is hosting at Francis Court, the amateur sleuth, with help from her clever dog Daisy and best friend Perry, must catch the killer before the partygoers find out and New Year's Eve is ruined.

Snow descends on Drew Castle in Scotland cutting the castle off and forcing Lady Beatrice along with Daisy her clever dog, and her best friends Perry and Simon to cooperate with boorish DCI Fitzwilliam to catch a killer before they strike again.

A murder at Gollingham Palace sparks a hunt to find the killer. For once, Lady Beatrice is happy to let DCI Richard Fitzwilliam get on with it. But when information comes to light that indicates it could be linked to her husband's car accident fifteen years ago, she is compelled to get involved. Will she finally find out the truth behind James's tragic death?

An unforgettable bachelor weekend for Perry filled with luxury, laughter, and an unexpected death.
Can Bea, Perry, and his hen's catch the killer before the weekend is over?

OTHER BOOKS BY HELEN GOLDEN

Bake Off Wars is being filmed on site at Francis Court and everyone is buzzing. But when much-loved pastry chef and judge, Vera Bolt, is found dead on set, can Bea, with the help of her best friend Perry, his husband Simon, and her cute little terrier, Daisy, expose the killer before the show is over?

Even in a charming seaside town, secrets don't stay buried for long as Bea and Perry discover when they uncover the remains of a chef who disappeared 3 years ago. As they unravel a web of professional rivalries and buried grudges, they must race against time to solve the murder before the grand opening of Simon's new restaurant.

Lady Beatrice's peaceful holiday in Portugal is shattered when a Hollywood star's husband is found dead. What appears to be an accident soon reveals itself as murder. Tasked with clearing an innocent woman's name, Bea and Rich must untangle a web of lies to uncover the truth before it's too late.

Perry is excited to be playing Algernon in The Importance of Being Ernest by Oscar Wilde. But disaster strikes during rehearsals, and a leading actor is killed. And it's no accident.
Can Bea and Perry sift through the petty jealousies and diva behaviour of the larger than life characters in the theatre company to unmask the culprit before Perry's acting debut is ruined?

www.ingramcontent.com/pod-product-compliance
Lightning Source LLC
Chambersburg PA
CBHW032018180726
48283CB00008B/2732